ALSO BY MARGOT BERWIN

Hothouse Flower and the Nine Plants of Desire

SCENT OF
DARKNESS

SCENT OF

DARKNESS

MARGOT BERWIN

PANTHEON BOOKS · NEW YORK

Copyright © 2013 by Margot Berwin

All rights reserved. Published in the United States by Pantheon Books,
a division of Random House, Inc., New York, and in Canada by
Random House of Canada Limited, Toronto.

Pantheon Books and colophon are registered trademarks of
Random House, Inc.

Library of Congress Cataloging-in-Publication Data
Berwin, Margot.
Scent of Darkness / Margot Berwin.
p. cm.
ISBN 978-0-307-90752-3
I. Title.
PS3602.E7697A7 2012
813'.6—DC23
2012011178

www.pantheonbooks.com

Jacket photograph: Captureworx/Millennium Images, U.K.
Jacket calligraphy by Nancy Howell
Jacket design by Emily Mahon

Printed in the United States of America
First Edition
2 4 6 8 9 7 5 3 1

For Lisa Levy, Sam Hiyate, and Jennifer Jackson

SCENT OF DARKNESS

1

My name is Eva, from the longer and more beautiful Evangeline. I had something very special once, something that I took for granted and lost. I set out to find it again, and as so often happens, it was right there in front of me. Or should I say it was right there inside of me, running through my veins like a blessing, or a plague.

☙

Jasmine smells like human flesh. Mix it with cumin, which smells like sweat, and you have the scent of sex. If you spread it on your body, watch out, you'll have sycophants all over the place, people crawling out of the woodwork to be close to you.

Human beings are defenseless against scent. They can't hide from it because they can't see it, or touch it, or hold it. All by itself it crawls into their brains, and by the time they're in love with it, or the person it's coming from, it's too late. They're tied to it forever, through the long, tight leash of memory.

I suppose what I'm trying to say is that a great scent, like a great love, can crash onto the shore of your life like a wave, creating either damage or change or, in my case, both.

What happened when I came across a scent like that was that I fell in love with two men at the same time, and one was pure evil, and one was good. It was an old-fashioned love triangle. A classic tale that came up roses, and jasmine, and, of course, tears.

So, my name is Eva, from the longer and more beautiful Evangeline. And for me, the scent I found held my past, present, and future in its ethereal little hand.

༄

I don't mean to be morbid and mostly I'm not, but it is possible to love someone evil. I know that for a fact. I wish I didn't, but wishing isn't going to change my story.

It happened during my eighteenth year, when I was too young to know that there are events and relationships that never go away. That you can never take back. That change you in ways over which you have no control.

My grandmother Louise, the person I was closest to, would say that none of that mattered anyway. That who we love isn't a question of good or evil, but one of scent.

"Scent can do crazy things to the mind," she said. "It can make us love people we shouldn't and turn away those we should. It can make us desire the child of a criminal and shun the overtures of a saint. Never open your legs for a man whose mind you love but only for the man whose scent you can't live without. That's the one you'll stay with forever."

I'd spent every summer of my childhood with Louise, but it was the summer of my eighteenth year that changed everything. That was the beginning of all the danger and the beauty and the blood.

2

Louise lived in the town of Cyril, which sat on a mountaintop in the westernmost part of New York State. It was a small town with only one road used for both directions, so it was said that the way in was also the way out.

The houses of Cyril were made of great gray stone slabs and had enormous fireplaces, which never seemed to make them warm. They stood in a circle, huddled together on the flat top of a low mountain overlooking an evergreen forest. Look up and the sun was shining. Look down and it was a midnight of trees.

The physical description of the town would not be important to my story except for the fact that Louise was an aromata, a master in the creation of scent. A sorceress of nothing, as she liked to call herself, for scent has no physical form.

She chose to live in Cyril because she liked when the wind whipped through the evergreens. When the cool smell of the pine needles blew through the windows of her house, which she called the Stone Crow, and erased any trace of her art from the noses of neighbors too interested.

"Never forget, Evangeline," she said, "those who make perfume consider themselves magicians of the highest order. They believe the scents they make possess the power to turn hate into love. Neutrality into desire. They don't share their choice of ingredients with anyone. They lock the doors to their laboratories with precision locks made by master craftsmen and later they kill those very same men so that no one will ever know the combination. Not a living soul."

"I'll remember that, Louise," I said.

I called her by her first name at her insistence. She thought "Grandmother" was too formal and put too many years between us, making it impossible for us to be friends.

"Put irises next to your mother's bed," she told me, "and she'll bring you a baby brother. Add a drop of lavender to the wash water and you'll dream of the man you'll love. Eucalyptus makes you taller, almondine fatter, and jasmine—oh, jasmine will wrap your entire life in a mystery."

"Do you believe that?" I asked.

"Not all of it. But it's true what they say about jasmine. If it comes from southern India, look out. Wear it often enough and I swear you won't recognize your own life. You'll be so confused about who you are you won't be able to pick your face out of a crowd in your own dream."

3

Louise didn't start out in Cyril. She was born in a small town called Fayetteville in south-central Louisiana. She was Louise from Louisiana, her very name inseparable from the thick, boggy, impenetrable swamp from which she came.

"People up north call it the bayou," she said, "when really it's a hundred different bayous, no two of them the same, and each one capable of destroying you in its own particular way. Some look shallow and harmless but they'll suck you under and hold you down in the mud till the very last breath comes out of your lungs. Others will sit there for decades, stagnant, mocking, taking a little bit more of your soul, year after year, like a man who doesn't love you back."

But in truth Louise from Louisiana loved the bayous and it was my fault that she ended up leaving her hometown.

When she turned sixty she left Louisiana and headed north for upstate New York. She moved in order to help out her only child, Loretta, who by that time had me and was living alone, a single mother in the borough of Brooklyn.

I had a father, I suppose everyone does, but I was the product of a lonely woman and a one-night stand. He was gone before the sperm hit the egg, as my mother liked to say.

The stranger who was my father did not leave me anything I could see in the mirror, and all Loretta could remember was that he had pork-chop sideburns, silver-rimmed aviator sunglasses, and he drank whiskey and Coca-Cola at the bar down the street. Oh, and his name was Ray, and he had a motorcycle, which he drove off on in the middle of that fated night of my conception.

Loretta was a strict Catholic, so getting rid of the pregnancy was out of the question, but she made sure to tell me often enough that she had never wanted children. That if it were not for me she would have forgotten about Ray immediately, referring to him not by his name, as I have, but simply as the worst thirty seconds of her life.

In the beginning Louise and my mother had a mutual fantasy that they would help each other out; Louise would go down to the city to babysit, and Loretta would make the occasional weekend trip to Cyril to do some shopping and small errands, maybe take Louise to the hairdresser every once in a while. But in the end the move was pointless. My mother never visited Cyril, not once, and Louise never went downstate either. She had left her beloved Louisiana for nothing.

Loretta, who was not particularly fond of Louise, put it this way: "Just because you're born into a particular family doesn't mean those people are your family. You share your blood and sometimes you have to accept that it's the only thing you'll ever have in common."

But no matter what Loretta said, Louise was much more than a bloodline to me. In truth, I liked her more than anyone else I knew. It may sound strange considering the difference in our ages, but it wasn't, and I wasn't. The two of us were amenable. Cut from the same cloth. Like two peas in the same damaged family pod.

We had a lot of things in common, Louise and I. For instance, we both liked to sleep late. I was a champion sleeper, gifted really— ten-, twelve-, even fourteen-hour stretches were nothing for me, and when I stayed with her she would let me go on and on, dreaming forever. We both understood that sleeping was a part of life exactly equal to being awake, while my mother thought it was something that should be limited, doled out, like long, hot showers, or affection.

She never ate in the morning, at least not during the prescribed breakfast eating hours, and neither did I. It was our least favorite meal of the day since it cut into the extra time we could be spending in bed, dreaming.

She didn't care what time I came home at night or who I hung around with, what I wore, or read. Part of the reason she trusted me so much was that she had her own life, which meant less time spent pondering mine.

We were both slim and too fragile in appearance, with slender hands and fine hair, which I wore straight down my back and Louise wove into a tall beehive, for height. She had a long aquiline nose, clear blue eyes, and lips like mine that were thin but not stern.

But more than anything else, we shared a certain darkness of spirit. A natural attraction for all things mysterious and unseen, even gory.

When I was ten I rose from my bed in the middle of the night during a terrible dream and ran across the room into a half-open door. The impact of the wood, a hard oak, made a deep gash over my left eye that bled down my face and onto my nightgown in big red raindrops.

Without any nervousness, maybe even with some small touch of happiness, Louise came out of her bedroom and pressed a washcloth against the flow. The cut was deep and the cloth was soaked before the bleeding could be stopped.

In the kitchen she took the bloody towel from my head and squeezed it out into an empty ice-cube tray. She stuck wooden ice-cream sticks into each little square and put it in the freezer.

"Bloodsicles," she said, "for the dogs."

We both took great delight in the creation of such an eccentric delicacy and although we had no dogs, the bloodsicles remain in the freezer to this day.

As the years went by she saved every drop of blood that came out of my body. Band-Aids and towels from cuts, scrapes, and falls were kept in jars and frozen forever. And I always remembered that she thought I was worth saving.

4

My mother was also dark in nature but her darkness was different than ours and had nothing to do with delight. Hers was the darkness of depression. The kind that made her sit night after night on the red couch in the living room with the red carpet drinking gin and tonics and smoking Camel filters. Her brown eyes were always wide open. Shocked that way, glued, eyelashes to forehead. She smoked and drank as if she were trying to speed up the process of death. As if she were attempting to give it a hand.

In the late spring of my seventeenth year I walked out of the last class of the semester and found her waiting outside of my school. She must have gotten there early, because she was parked in the best spot, right in front of the doors, sitting in her impossible-to-miss vintage silver Buick Skylark from the 1970s.

I stood on the front steps and watched her from a few yards away. She inhaled from a cigarette but then she had to yawn, so instead of blowing the smoke out of her lungs, she just opened her mouth wide and it came out in a slow cloud that hid her face. It was a good thing too, that cloud, because her skin was nothing much to look at, mottled and sagging from its constant contact with smoke.

From a certain angle she reminded me of a slot machine with wrinkles that went straight up and down her cheeks deep enough to slip quarters into. Sometimes I stared at her face and wondered, if I slipped a coin into a wrinkle and pulled her forearm down, would she cough up coins or would dollar signs spin in her irises?

"Get in," she said. "Your stuff is already packed up in the back."

"You went through my closet?"

"We're going to miss the bus."

"How do you know what I want to take?"

"You packed it yourself."

"How do you know I was finished?"

"I don't. But I do know there's only one bus between now and Wednesday and you're going to be on it."

My mother was forever in a hurry to get rid of me. The very thing she was not able to do in the beginning.

I hunched down in the iron tank that was the Skylark. We drove in silence to the bus station, where she lit up and then handed me a ticket and some money.

I rested my suitcase on its wheels and waved at the back of the car as she pulled away. She saw me in the rearview mirror and hung two fingers out of the window with the cigarette in between them as a form of goodbye.

It was a strange thought to have about my own mother, but watching her leave in a cloud of exhaust fumes and ash, I had a feeling she wasn't going to live a very long life. I would find out later that I had the right thought about the wrong person.

5

Louise met me on the other side, so to speak. I held her slender hand in mine as we walked onto the main street of Cyril. I loved that walk through town, rolling my suitcase behind me, shedding the city with each step, soaking in the clear, country air. Those were often the best moments of the summer, those few blocks when the potential of July and August spread out before me, and the school year, finished just hours ago, was already a thing of the past.

We walked by a movie theater, a butcher shop with a faint smell of blood coming from an open window, a gas station, a bakery, and a pub. Cyril was a town with just one of everything. It was child-like in that way. Undeveloped, but with all of the things it needed to survive.

Louise and I stopped at the coffee shop on our way to her house. It was almost empty except for her best friend, Rosemary, who was waiting for us as she did every summer.

During the winters back in Brooklyn I tried to put the thought of Rosemary out of my mind. She was old and so thin that whenever I hugged her I felt like I was slipping my hands right through her skin and holding on to her beating heart.

Her pale eyes were cold and unrevealing, but she was gifted at reading the tarot cards, so while she herself was impossible to figure out, she could tell me anything I wanted to know about my own life.

Once, a long time ago, she'd had "the High Priestess" tattooed on her back. For years, well into her seventies, she walked around Cyril in nothing but a bathing-suit top and shorts. She was so unself-conscious about the appearance of her body; it was both charming and disturbing at the same time.

But now in her very old age Rosemary was always cold. Each day she left her house wearing every single piece of clothing she owned. Sweater over sweater over sweater until the last one could barely fit over her shoulders and pretty much just lay on top of her body, periodically dropping to the floor. The funny thing was that she complained about her back. She said it bothered her all the time. Personally I didn't think all those sweaters piled up on top of it were helping, but I kept quiet. I'm not sure if she knew it, but she looked as if she had a hump, as if she were aiming for the kind of look most people try to avoid at all cost.

"Pick that up, would you?" Rosemary said from her chair.

It was her last layer, a black, fuzzy sweater covered in bits and pieces of lint.

"It's not going to make you any warmer than the first twenty," I said.

"I'm older than you think, Evangeline. There are spots where my skin is just about worn off and little bits of bone are exposed to the air. On a windy day I feel like more and more of me is being blown away."

I bent down to pick up the sweater and when I stood up she was moving the napkins, water glasses, and salt shaker to one side of the table and spreading out the tarot cards. It was how we began each summer. No matter where we were when we first saw each other, Rosemary had me pick a card.

I looked over the deck spread across the table like a wave. I wasn't a true believer but I have to admit it gave me a little thrill to play with fate. I waited for the moment of clarity that always came when faced with the tarot and picked up the last card at the very end of the deck, at the edge of the table.

"Strange," said Rosemary, "most people pick from the center. Do you want to try again, sweetheart?"

"I want my card."

Rosemary looked over at Louise.

"Don't blame me if you don't like what I tell your granddaughter. The girl picked from the end of the line."

I put the card faceup on the table.

"The upside-down Magician," she said, "an interesting card."

"Good or bad?"

"Neither one nor the other. It's what I call a damned if you do, damned if you don't card."

She picked a piece of lint off the arm of her sweater and watched it trail to the floor. I could tell that she was killing time, procrastinating about the Magician.

"Well, sweetheart," she said, "the good news is that you're going to meet a man. He'll be an older man with words, lots of words, like little bits of paradise falling off of his tongue. He'll be able to convince you of just about anything. Things you would never do in the normal course of your lifetime."

"The bad news?"

"He's going to mislead you, that I can tell you for sure. If you follow him, you'll be going down the wrong road. One you'll never be able to get off of entirely and may regret forever."

"And if I don't?"

"Then there are things you won't learn that you're supposed to know. Difficulties you'll avoid but at the high cost of wisdom lost." Rosemary took a long drink of water. "Like I said, damned if you do, damned if you don't."

Personally I thought the upside-down Magician was beautiful. It meant that I would have a man in my life, something I'd never had before, even in the beginning.

I held the card in my hand, turning it over and over between my fingers, watching the Magician stand on his head and then right himself again while the waiter stood next to our table and listed the specials of the day. The spinning of the card was hypnotic and his voice sounded deep and sonorous and far away.

༄

Minutes passed before I pulled my mind off the Magician and looked up. The waiter was an older boy with beautiful skin that was hard to miss. Pale and so taut it seemed to pull his eyes and his cheekbones back toward his ears as if he were facing a strong wind. His hair was shiny and black and it moved whenever he did like ripples of dark lake water. He wore a black T-shirt, jeans, and work boots, and on the inside of his forearm was a beautiful blue star tattoo as if a part of the nighttime sky had fallen onto his arm and stayed there.

Rosemary whispered in my ear.

"That's not the one the upside-down Magician spoke of," she said. "He's much too young, and it's too soon."

She didn't need to tell me what I already knew. The waiter wasn't the older, magnetic stranger I was destined to meet. He was the boy who was out of my league. The boy with the long, shiny hair and high cheekbones that I would never get to talk to. If he were less beautiful I might wonder about him later; what his name was and if we would run into each other in town over the summer. But considering what he looked and sounded like I was free to forget him, knowing that he would do the same about me.

Louise watched me watch the waiter and then she leaned in close.

"Love is an olfactory experience," she said, "not a choice, like people want to think it is. So don't waste your time worrying about who's better looking. It has little meaning in the world of desire."

"He's from the next town over," Rosemary said, "and I'm pretty sure he goes to college in New Orleans. That's what I hear from the grapevine anyway."

"I've seen him around Cyril, off and on since he was a little boy," said Louise. "He's all grown up now, just like you."

I thought she sounded sad about the age of the waiter.

"He makes me think about the greatest perfumer I've ever known," she said, "a woman from Fayetteville, Louisiana, my hometown. A Cajun lady who mixed potions into scents so powerful they could make ants stand up on their hind legs and dance around in sheer joy waiting for just one drop of her sweet sweat to fall."

"What did she smell like?"

"Like time passing. And life going by."

Louise smelled the skin on the inside of her arm.

"A scent should have a certain melancholia, a sadness for a desire that will never be met, a person who got away, or a thing that can never be had. All the great perfumes contain this feeling. It's what gives them their depth. Every summer when you get off of that bus, a year older, a few inches taller, I can smell the scent of time clinging to you, closing over your body like scar tissue."

We left the coffee shop and I didn't look back at the waiter, and I was sure he didn't look at me.

On the way home, Rosemary took my hand, and it was true that I could feel the bones and joints of her fingers as if I were holding on to a skeleton with just some little bit of skin attached to keep her from being unsightly.

But it was Louise who seemed ill at ease, or simply ill. She moved slowly and the air around her body seemed tired. When I was near her I couldn't shake the thought of the scent of time passing.

6

We walked until we reached the dead end of a cul-de-sac made dark in the middle of the afternoon by overhanging weeping willow trees. Rainwater dripped off the branches like an unfriendly chill on a June day. A low brick wall with an arched iron gate stood in front of her house, the Stone Crow.

Louise wasn't severe by nature, but she did choose her home because of its off-putting characteristics. Except for Rosemary she did not want company and she wasn't neighborly. She believed that life was short and socializing was for time wasters and people who didn't have anything better to do.

She opened the gate with a skeleton key and as we walked up the path to the door it slammed shut behind us, metal on metal. Smoke came out of the chimney, making the air around the house smell comforting, like cedar, but the great gray stone slabs were cold and forbidding. They appeared haphazard, as if they'd been blown up out of the dirt during an earthquake and had landed one on top of the other, by sheer luck, in the shape of a house. Large pieces of slate and granite, extra building stones, were strewn over the grass of the front lawn like a graveyard.

I braced myself as she opened the front door. No matter how many years I'd been coming to the Stone Crow, walking into it for the first time each summer was like a slap in the face.

Louise was capable of creating any scent in the world. She could make a room smell like winter or innocence, eggshells, guilt, or dissatisfaction. But that summer she chose the scent of death for the long dark hallways and rooms of her home.

"Jasmine smells like the body in its final hours," she said. "Like the sweet, sweet scent of decay. Get used to it, Evangeline, and death will never surprise you."

We walked inside, through a narrow entranceway into the kitchen. It was painted yellow in an attempt at cheerfulness that didn't work.

I parted the curtains above the sink and looked out into the yard. It had a strange, overgrown beauty that no manicured lawn could match. A thorny mass of rosebushes, high, uncut grass, long and bright green with pale, dried-out tips, lilac trees, bees, birds, and butterflies all mixing together made it look desirable but impossible to wade into, like a painting in a museum.

Louise took a piece of cured fish from the refrigerator and brought it over to the wooden table in the center of the room. The mixed scent of seawater and jasmine was nauseating. I bent over the fish. The scales had miniature rainbow patterns that were strangely reflective, as if they were holding on to the memory of water.

She took my hand and pressed it onto the fish. It was firm and soft, with a great, living feeling. She blew on my skin and when it was dry she traced the white salt lines with her fingertips.

"The salt dries in perfect shapes as if the designs were preordained by the sea itself."

Two sharp teeth sat in the center of my palm.

"What do they mean?" I asked.

"Nothing good," she said.

The beautiful fish made me strangely sad and so that night I stayed hungry. I thought about how each summer was the same. I got off the bus and walked down Main Street, where everything was bright and sunny and then, just hours later, I had salt teeth in the palm of my hand.

7

We walked up the wide stone stairway to the top floor of the Stone Crow. Louise opened a door and a rush of damp, cold air spread out into the hallway. The scent that came out of the room was incredible and hideous. A combination of wood smoke and birthing blood I remembered from a dog in labor in a neighbor's backyard.

She went inside and left me standing in the hall with my suitcase, freezing and unsure whether to knock or leave her alone.

"Go to your room and put your things away," she said from the other side.

But I was unable to move, transfixed, as I was year after year, by the possibility of what lay behind that door to the only room in Louise's house that I was never allowed to enter.

She stepped out and stood in front of me once again.

She hung her head and closed her eyes.

"It's always the same thing," she said.

"I know."

"There's nothing for you to see in there. I'm not hiding anything or keeping a secret. I've told you before and I guess I have to tell you again, although I wish I didn't."

I sat down on top of my suitcase and listened to Louise recite the same sentences I'd heard for so many summers in a row.

"It's an empty round white room that will not make you feel good about yourself," she said. "You won't find anything inside that you'll like or even remotely enjoy. Its emptiness will only make you feel lonely and that loneliness will stick to you for a long time, weighing you down and causing you pain. Do you want that?"

"I want to decide for myself."

"Let me explain it to you this way," she said. "Most artists make something from nothing. They take a blank page and a pen and they create a song or a poem, or they stand in front of a canvas and make a painting filled with light and life, or darkness and hate and misery. I do the opposite. I take something that's already in existence, a flower or a fruit, an animal, a bone, a tooth, or a heart, something that has weight and mass and is tangible here on this earth, something that you can hold and touch and care about, and then I turn it into nothing. Ephemera. Antimatter. I create scent, Evangeline, a thing of great beauty that is nothing in and of itself. There is no form, no density. So you see there is nothing in there for you to hold on to. There is no take-away to that space. It is profoundly and disturbingly empty. I've been walking into that room for years and you should know that at this point the sadness of it never leaves me. I couldn't shake it if I tried."

She opened the door but I held on to her arm.

"I've seen you take Rosemary inside."

"She is old," said Louise. "She has witnessed the death of people she loves, she has dealt with the sickness and diseases of age with dignity. She has borne children and watched them leave home and make mistakes and even die. Rosemary can handle the coldness and the sadness with equanimity. And because of what she has already been through, I don't have to feel any guilt for bringing her inside. To take someone young like you into that room would be a mistake. Not just for you, but for myself as well."

"What are you doing in there? Can I ask you that?"

"I'm working on change," she said, and then she slid back in and locked the door behind her.

It was another summer that I would remain outside, in the hallway. I hated the thought but I had to wonder whether part of the reason I went to Cyril every year was the lure of the white room. I went for Louise, of course, but it was as if there was a part of her I would never get to know. It created a type of imbalance in me. A desire. A nervousness. I imagined it was like knowing, without any proof, that someone you love has another lover.

8

The summer came and went and back home with Loretta it rained almost every night during the February of my senior year. The days were gray and misty, but by ten o'clock each night a strange and persistent wintertime thunder rolled in and the raindrops began.

Some people love falling asleep to the sound of rain. They fall fast and easy and sleep long and well, but I'm not one of those people. The drip, drip, dripping tortures me. Each ping against the metal of the air-conditioning unit or the glass of the windowpane makes my blood bounce. I find myself wide-eyed, my body primed and waiting for the next drop to fall. It's as if I can hear each one individually and sleep becomes a distant dream.

It was raining the day Loretta told me that Louise was sick. We were driving down the highway on our way to somewhere that no longer matters when she gave me the news. I wanted to look into her eyes to see how bad it was but she didn't take them off the road. I could not blame her. It was cold and cloudy with drops coming down so fast it was as if we had driven into the sea.

We pulled off the highway and stopped, waiting for the deluge to die down. The sound of the raindrops pounding on the roof and the hood made me feel more agitated than I already was. I rolled down the window and let the scent of the storm fill the car.

"How sick is she?" I asked.

"Too sick for a hospital to help her," said Loretta. "She waited too long."

Now I knew why I hated the sound of the rain. All along it had been a premonition of the end of Louise.

The torrent slowed and we drove back onto the highway. I leaned over and stuck my head out into the swift, cool air. I could hear Loretta in the distance telling me to close the window, but I couldn't. The world rushed by and the scent of rain brought back Louise's words.

"Jasmine smells like death," she'd said. "Like the sweet, sweet scent of decay. Get used to it, Evangeline, and death will never surprise you."

I had spent the entire summer living under the heavy scent of jasmine, breathing in its molecules of indoles in every room of the Stone Crow. But I had not listened to her advice.

When we were home I opened the door to my bedroom. It was freezing inside. I had left the window open ever so slightly to let out some of the heat from the radiator, but still, it was so cold that no one had to tell me that Louise had passed. I sat down on my bed and for the first time I understood the emptiness of the white room. I knew the sadness of nothingness that Louise had tried to tell me about. I was perhaps ready for that room only now that she was gone.

Because she was old I had already spent many nights in bed, imagining her death, steeling myself ahead of time against a world without her in it. But just then I knew there was no way to prepare for such a thing, because the universe becomes a different place with each person who steps in or out.

I was told that she died of heart failure but I had a hard time accepting that, as I could not imagine her failing at anything. I spent a lot of time walking around by myself or sitting in my room alone trying to figure out the true cause of her death. She had told me she was working on change and I wondered whether she had succeeded and simply changed herself right out of this world.

Her death became like a mystery to me although it didn't seem that way to anyone else. To the people who knew her she was an old woman who died of heart failure, which is really old age, after living a long life.

I blamed myself for not being in Cyril when her time came. For not knowing exactly how it happened, the way I would have if I'd been with her, or if anyone had been with her at all. That was the part that bothered me the most. That she was alone in that great gray house when she passed. The only thing I could do was to be there for her now. I would go up to Cyril and make all the funeral arrangements myself.

"You don't have to go," Loretta said. "Rosemary's offered to take care of everything."

"No, *you* don't have to go," I said. "I have to."

"I don't want you to feel pressured."

"Love doesn't feel like pressure to me."

I didn't expect my mother to go to Cyril, not even for Louise's funeral. She lived her life as if she were on a moving sidewalk in an airport. Things and people, even those—or especially those—she was closest to, passed by her in a flash. They were interesting to look at but they held no lasting meaning in her life.

9

I spent the morning of Louise's funeral sitting in Rosemary's kitchen staring out the window, which faced the backyard of the Stone Crow. The garden was wilder than ever and the lilac bushes had grown tall. Louise would have appreciated the height.

"I have something to show you," Rosemary said. "Come with me, dear."

She had never called me "dear" and it frightened me to no end. Rosemary was capable of stupendous acts of freakishness that I was not in the mood for, but was also too sad to ward off. I picked up a sweater that had fallen off her back as she walked down the hallway toward her bedroom and hung it over the railing.

Her room smelled like mothballs, a scent I found sickening. I sat down on the very edge of her bed, repulsed by her camphor-soaked blankets, touching as little of them as possible. The bed squeaked even though I sat on the farthest corner, an outpost really, some-place I was sure no one had ever been before. I stared through the window at Louise's house feeling as agitated as I did in a rainstorm, while Rosemary searched through her closet.

By the time she emerged the sun was in a different part of the sky.

She rolled an old wheelchair to the edge of the bed. The wheels were dry and rusty and the gray seat was torn and had an upside-down paper bag sitting on top of it.

"Pick it up," she said.

I cannot describe how much I hated that moment. I lifted it off the seat, pinching it between two fingernails and touching it as little as possible.

Under the bag Louise's beehive was sitting on the wheelchair as perfectly coiffed as when she was alive. Rosemary had chopped off my grandmother's hair and put it in her closet. Small flying insects circled it as if it were a living thing with Louise still attached, underneath.

"Hair never grows old or dies," Rosemary said, stroking the hive. "I have the locks of all my loved ones who have passed, right here in this room. It's my own little way of keeping them close. Look at it dear. Isn't it beautiful? Go ahead and smell it if you want to."

Rosemary leaned over and breathed in Louise's hair.

"Would you like to have it?" she asked.

I bent over the beehive and looked down through the hole in the top. It was a nesty, dead-looking thing. Not at all the way I wanted to remember my grandmother.

⌇

A month after her funeral I found out that Louise had left her house to me.

My mother handed me the keys.

"It's all yours," she said. "When school's done you can go up there and clean the place out."

"You mean I can go through my favorite person in the entire

world's very precious things, and decide what to keep and what to get rid of," I said.

"Yep. That's what I said. Clean it out."

10

It was the last day of my last year of high school when I went back up to Cyril. It was a strange experience arriving at the bus depot without Louise there to take my hand.

I walked alone along Main Street wheeling my luggage behind me. Everything was just as it always was—the coffee shop, the gas station, the butcher, the pub. But really, nothing was the same.

The air felt still, as if the pine trees had stopped moving since Louise had died. As if the town itself and the forest below were in mourning.

It would be a long time until someone like her came along, I thought, and everything here knows it.

At the end of the cul-de-sac the Stone Crow stood as it always had. Inanimate objects are strange that way. They keep their exact form no matter what happens. They just keep doing what they were built to do. I mean, Louise died inside that house and yet it registered absolutely nothing. It stood resolutely on, waiting for the next person to move in and animate its hallways and rooms and then die somewhere inside.

I opened the gate and walked through the front yard wishing Louise had been buried there, underneath one of the extra stone slabs. I put the key in the door and gave it a shove. It didn't move an inch. It was a heavy, arched brown wooden door set tightly into the surrounding stone and I wondered how Louise, so tiny, had managed to push it open, day after day, year after year. I hadn't bothered to ask, and maybe it was a small concern, but it was just one more thing I would never know about my grandmother.

I put my suitcase down and pushed with my entire body until the house revealed itself to me. It smelled of decay just as it had the summer before, but now I wasn't sure whether it was the jasmine or Louise's death that caused the scent.

It was warm inside, almost lifelike, and as I walked down the front hallway I ran my fingertips along the gray stone wall half expecting it to move in and out with breath.

A light was on in the kitchen and I could smell burning wood from the fireplace in the great room. I thought that Rosemary had prepared the house for my arrival, but as I continued down the hallway I began to wonder if it was Louise herself. Perhaps she hadn't died at all. It was irrational, I knew, but I left my suitcase where I stood and walked toward the light. I don't know whether it was hope or loneliness, but I was sure I was going to see Louise at the head of the long table in the middle of the kitchen.

ॐ

It was a shock to see the boy from the coffee shop. The one with the tight, pale skin and the long dark hair. He was at the very table where Louise should have been, surrounded by books and papers spread out all around him as if he had been there for a long, long time.

We stared, both of us visibly upset to see another person in the house. He was probably afraid of being caught while I was weighed down with the disappointment that he was not Louise.

We waited in unison, if two people can do such a thing, for the other one to speak. I looked straight at him, hard, with one hand on either side of the doorframe, trying to conjure a toughness I did not feel. It worked anyway and he put both of his hands up on either side of his head, palms facing out toward me in a position of surrender.

"I haven't touched a thing in here," he said. "I've never even been in another room in the house, except to light the fire. I knew the old lady died and I thought the place was empty. I came here just one time to study and it was so quiet that I kept coming back. I knew it wasn't right, but it was just so quiet."

It was the same deep voice and shimmering black hair I remembered from the coffee shop, except now he was in Louise's house, and for just one moment he seemed like a young, beautiful reincarnation of her, sent just for me.

"It's my grandmother's house," I said. "Her name was Louise Lennon and she died four months ago, in the winter, of possible heart failure."

"I'm so sorry," he said. "I remember her, I do. She was a good customer. I liked her very much."

"Everyone did."

Talking about Louise clobbered me, stiffening my internal organs, closing my chest and making it hard to inhale.

"Did you go to her funeral?" I asked. "I don't remember seeing you there."

"I had to study," he said.

"The rest of the town went."

"I heard about it, if that helps."

"What did you hear?"

"That the pews were scented with jasmine from the south of India."

He made neat piles of his papers and books and slipped them into his backpack.

"I didn't mean to intrude."

Brushing past me on his way out he smelled like musk. Like something Louise called an animalic, the scent from the gland of a male deer.

He turned around in the middle of the hallway.

"My name's Gabriel. I thought you should know since I've been inside of your grandmother's house."

Like the archangel, I thought, the impact of Loretta's Catholicism making a rare appearance in my mind. I made a mental note to look up the angel Gabriel and see what deeds he had done to deserve his angel status.

When Gabriel was gone his glandular scent, earthy and sweet, lingered in the room. I remembered Louise telling me that a good scent should not smell like a perfume, but like nature itself, including all aspects of the natural world, dark and animal as well as light and floral. "Love includes the bad as well as the good," she'd said, "the evil as well as the kind, and so should the scent that induces it."

I ran my hands over the old wood of the kitchen table. I could feel her presence in every knot and groove and I was glad that someone had been in the house keeping it warm, not just for me, but also for her. For whatever was left of her in the cracks and crevices, in the floorboards and the walls and the mirrors.

I went into my room and emptied my suitcase on the bed. I put my things away in the drawers I'd used for so many summers and lay down under the maroon-and-teal patchwork blanket I'd slept under for so many years that its scent was the same as my own skin, and finally closed my eyes.

I wanted to think about Louise, I wanted to dream about her and bring her back to life in that way, but instead I lay awake with a picture of Gabriel in my mind. I thought: I'm supposed to meet someone named Gabriel, like the angel, because he's here to tell me that Louise is okay, and that it's all right to die.

11

Louise claimed that sleeping in a stone house had a positive effect on her body because the stones had accumulated energy from the earth over thousands of years. I had never believed her, but that first morning alone in the Stone Crow, I felt unusually awake.

I walked down the long, wide, sweeping staircase to the first floor. She must have had it built in this way because she came from the South, where the width of a staircase had meaning. The stairs themselves probably missed her southernness and her slow, debutante-like walk. I'm sure they resented my clipped and quick northeastern gait, feeling their own graciousness going to waste.

I looked at every painting on the way down. Louise had had portraits done of all of her friends, but with the exception of myself there were no family members included, not even my mother.

By the time I reached the bottom of the stairs there was a knock on the door. The timing was perfect, just like in the movies, as though someone was waiting for my foot to touch the last step.

Gabriel stood outside on the porch. It was drizzling and his black hair was covered with a slight mist that made it look gray. For a moment I thought he was very old and that I had slept for a hundred years.

"I meant to ask you yesterday," he said, "what are *you* doing here?"

"I'm here for the house," I said. "My grandmother left it for me to take care of."

He was quiet and I watched the rainwater cling to him. I had hated the rain for so long, and now I felt jealous of it too.

"I know this is a lot to ask, but would it be possible for me to study here? There are five of us at my house and it's noisy all the time. Incredibly, indescribably noisy."

I was silent.

"I'm neat, I'm quiet, I respect other people's stuff and I make great coffee, which I get for free from the coffee shop even though I don't work there anymore. Kind of a lifelong benefit, like Social Security."

"What are you studying?"

"I'm a medical student at Tulane. I come back summers because I'm not built for the heat in New Orleans. I've got thick, northeastern blood."

"Louise was from Fayetteville, outside of New Orleans."

"I know it well."

"What kind of medicine are you studying?" I asked.

"Hematology, the study of blood, or maybe geriatrics."

I looked again at his hair, gray from the mist, and I thought that maybe it was the better choice.

"So you're interested in keeping people alive?"

"For as long as possible."

"How long is that?" I asked, stepping aside and letting him in.

"In the best of circumstances, good nutrition, air quality, water, medicine, and love, maybe a hundred and twenty years."

"And with your help?"

"Could be a little longer," he said.

Gabriel spread his books across the kitchen table in the exact pattern they had been in the day before. I would not have remembered that kind of detail except that I had noticed two of his textbooks hanging off the edge of the table in such a way that a single breath at just the right angle would have made them fall. Something like that took practice and I wondered just how much time he had spent in the house. It didn't matter, though, because just then he pulled his dark green sweater over his head. Now he was sitting at the table in a black T-shirt. Now I would never get anything done or be able to think about anything else maybe ever again.

He picked up a pen and I saw the small, blue star tattoo on the inside of his arm, the one that looked like a fallen star. It was on the tender, pale part between the elbow and the wrist.

He followed my eyes to his arm.

"It's a birthmark," he said.

I moved in closer. "It's perfect. No one is born with something like that."

"I was lucky."

I backed away from him and his lucky birthmark. It unnerved me. I had never seen something so well formed that was essentially a deformity.

"I'm not the first person to be born like this," he said. "It happens sometimes."

"I'm not a big believer in things just happening."

I picked up a sponge from the countertop. A part of me was tempted to try to wash the thing off his arm but instead I went into the living room to clean.

It was chilly in the house even though it was summer, so I started a fire in the great room and immediately fell asleep on the couch.

⁊

"Evangeline, Evangeline, wake up!"

It was Gabriel, kneeling next to me on the floor.

"What is it?"

He leaned over me to whisper in my ear.

"Shush . . . it's okay," he said. "There's someone at the door. I can tell them to go away if you want me to."

I crawled up through the twisting, turning gray lobes of my brain and forced my eyes open, but when I did the great room was empty and Gabriel was not whispering in my ear.

I had the sad feeling of waking up after dreaming about someone who has left or died, dreaming that they're still here and that you're doing things together and that you *are* together. It seemed that I missed Gabriel without ever knowing him and before he was even gone. Or maybe he was just a substitute for Louise and I was grieving all wrong. Replacing the people I cared about with other, newer people instead of getting the original death out of my system.

I knew that by the time I was old all the people I had not grieved for were going to be stacked up, one on top of the other, in my mind, waiting for their little piece of my grief. I felt tired just thinking about it.

12

After that first day, Gabriel and I fell into a pattern. He would come over every morning and make coffee and we would sit at the long kitchen table chatting about the house, Louise, the science of aging, and the study of blood. I knew that I liked him because I gave up my marathon sleeping for him. He was the first person I met besides Louise who was better than dreaming.

While he studied, I would go through her belongings. Louise was a person who kept everything she had ever gotten her hands on that she liked in any way. I was the opposite. I couldn't wait to get rid of things. I got a special feeling from throwing things away—the kind of feeling other people get from shopping sprees.

At first I only touched her things, running my fingers over them without moving a single item out of its place, waiting for my desire to throw away to kick in. But in the end it never did and not a single book, cup, shirt, or sheet was moved from its original space. Everything would remain exactly as she left it. Exactly as it should be.

When I was a child and my room was messy my mother would empty the closets and the drawers onto the floor with such vehemence it was as if she hated the objects in my room, as if they had somehow personally offended her. Louise, on the other hand, lifted up each object and dusted it off as if she had made it herself. In deference to her style I cleaned her things with care and placed them back into the position in which I'd found them.

When Gabriel needed a break from studying he helped me clean. As the summer went on his breaks became so frequent I came to believe that he was more interested in Louise's belongings than in medicine.

"Did you notice the signs on the doors?" he asked.

I had to admit that I hadn't.

"Her rooms are named and arranged in time," he said, "like chronological events or Italian frescoes where a whole story is composed in one painting, past, present, and future."

I scanned my mind for an image of an Italian fresco. In what corner of my brain could it possibly reside?

"This one here, *Terminus,* means 'the end,'" he said.

"That's the room where Rosemary found her, after she died."

"And this one, *Medius,* means 'middle' or 'center.' Maybe for the middle period of her life. And that one, *Originis,* means 'beginning.'"

"And this?" I asked, pointing to the door of the workroom, which read *Mutatio.*

"Change, mutation, or transformation."

"Louise was a generous person, but that room is the one thing she never offered."

"Things change," said Gabriel.

"How do you know?"

"Because the door says *Mutatio.*"

13

On my fifth Sunday I dressed for church, thinking it might be a good idea for the people of Cyril to see my face. It was a small town and I didn't want them worrying about the girl living in Louise Lennon's house who never stepped into the light of day.

I chose a deep maroon wraparound dress, dark enough to be considered a mourning color in honor of Louise, but with just enough light to signal that I was feeling okay and moving past her death—as if such a thing were possible. I wore her favorite scent, jasmine from India. Not from the south, she said, but from the south of *India.* Wear it often enough and it will make a mystery of your life, she told me, and even though it was the first time I'd had it on my skin I believed it was already working.

"It's your grandmother who died, not your husband," said Rosemary, sitting next to me. "Stop acting like an old widow and come around more often. Louise would never want to see you like this."

She had a point. Louise would hate that I was staying inside all day, but only because it was the warmest month of the year, the one that smelled the sweetest from all the flowers in bloom.

I closed my eyes and pictured Gabriel sitting at the kitchen table surrounded by books the first day I'd come back to Cryil after Louise had died. I remembered how sure I was, walking down the hallway, that she was still alive. It may have been the silence of the church and the scent of jasmine on my wrists that created the thought, but once it entered my mind there was nothing I could do to make it leave. The thought was that Louise had willed Gabriel to me. That he was as much a part of my inheritance as the Stone Crow itself: a living, breathing, posthumous present from her to me. She did not leave me alone. She left me alone *with* Gabriel.

My eyes had been closed and I opened them just as Father Madrid walked up to the pulpit to begin his sermon. He was the only priest Cyril had had for as long as I'd been spending my summers with Louise, and I trusted him because she did.

"He's not a great man," she'd said, "but he does his best. He has the scent of someone who gives it their all but does not succeed. It's the scent of the fig. It bursts into bloom with so much vigor, and it tries so hard to hang on, but it dies as soon as it leaves the vine. And that's what will become of Father Madrid too. He'll try to hang on but he won't make it. A rush, maybe of insight, and then a swift death. One of the sweetest scents on earth, the fig."

꒳

"Today begins our discussion of the archangel Gabriel," said Father Madrid.

I felt the nylon of my dress stick to my back.

"He's going to talk about Gabriel," I whispered to Rosemary.

"Yes he is. The beautiful angel Gabriel."

"That's the name of the boy at the coffee shop."

Rosemary looked at me, full of pity.

"Don't let death make you see patterns where there are none."

⚮

"Gabriel will give you things you never expected to receive in this lifetime. He will take you places in love that you cannot imagine. Gabriel will haunt you. Gabriel can save you. Gabriel will make you want to live forever. Gabriel will make you wish you were dead."

I looked around the packed church for *my* Gabriel.

Father Madrid continued.

"Gabriel is the messenger of God and the angel of death. How can one being be both of those things?

"Gabriel signifies duality, complication, perplexity; the true human condition in the form of an angel.

"How many of you have acted like Gabriel in your day-to-day life? On the one hand finding a special person to love and on the other hand bringing pain and heartache to that very same person?

"On the one hand loving someone new and exciting. And on the other knowing that that very love brings destruction and hurt to others, who feel abandoned by you as you live only for your new love, and brings pain to those who desire your beloved for themselves.

"How many of you are like the angel Gabriel?"

The low sound of "amen" echoed through the room.

"There is always duality. We are all, each and every one of us, the angel Gabriel, and he is all of us too."

I sat in the pew and all I could think of was my Gabriel, right now, sitting at the kitchen table studying medicine. He would become a messenger to the sick, letting them know whether or not they would live, or maybe keeping them alive for longer periods of time. He would also be the angel of death for so many others when he had to tell them that they would not survive.

Gabriel, I thought, my angel. My gift. My inheritance.

14

Rosemary and I sat down at Louise's favorite table near the swinging kitchen doors of the coffee shop. I studied the menu as if it were a textbook, not wanting to look up at the waiter for fear that it would somehow be Gabriel, back at work, and not at the Stone Crow, where I was sure he belonged.

It turned out that I had nothing to worry about since the new waiter was a waitress.

"I'll have two eggs with bacon, and white toast," said Rosemary.

"You?" she asked me. Not *And you,* or *What would you like to have,* but just *You?*

I stared at her. She wore a short, old white T-shirt with a faded black yin/yang sign. She had long, dark hair, and low black jeans. She was skinny and her clothes looked perfect on her body, as if she could walk out of the coffee shop and right onto a stage where her band would be going on in five minutes to a packed house.

I turned to Rosemary. "Who is she?"

"Rayanne? She's a neighborhood girl. A lovely girl. Gabriel chose her as his replacement. He said she would be just as good as he was, but if you ask me she's even better."

Rayanne came back with the food and coffee. As she bent over the table I noticed that she had ridges in her lips as if she didn't drink enough water, which was strange for someone who put glasses of it in front of people all day long.

She placed the food down with obvious care. She didn't slam the plates or create a lot of noise. It was the same with the coffee, not a drop splashed over the side of the cup.

She looked at me.

"I'll see you later," she said.

I felt my stomach muscles bunch together and I wanted to ask her what she meant, what possible reason she could have for seeing me later, but she was already walking away and all I saw was her black jeans with the outline of a pack of cigarettes in the left back pocket and her long hair that swung back and forth, brushing the indentations of her waist.

15

They came to the Stone Crow looking like a pair of tall, thin, stylish people. Shiny people is what they were, both of them polished, clean, and good-looking.

I should not have been surprised to see them together and I wasn't, really. I was horrified, disappointed, mortified, upset, nauseous, and wanting to go back to bed. But I was not surprised.

"Rayanne has the day off," said Gabriel. "She offered to help us clean."

He seemed nervous, with a ripple in his usually sonorous voice, which made me queasy.

"Another pair of hands can't hurt," she said, holding up her own and looking into my eyes.

It was not a look that made me like her more.

I took Gabriel's arm and walked him from the hallway into the kitchen, away from Rayanne.

"I don't feel comfortable with a stranger looking through Louise's things."

"Gabriel is a stranger too," Rayanne said, coming up right behind us. "You just met him, didn't you?"

"Gabriel belongs in the house."

"What?" they said at the same time.

My discomfort with Rayanne was obvious and Gabriel walked her outside while I stood in the kitchen. I didn't turn around to look at them. I didn't want to see what was between them. I did not want to know if he took her hand or kissed her at the front door.

There are times when I'm utterly sure that it's best not to know what you're up against, as it keeps you from feeling crushed inside.

"Rayanne's a nice person," Gabriel said. "She's a careful, gracious person. She would never steal Louise's stuff or even talk about it to other people. She's not like that at all."

"It was out of respect," I said as firmly as possible. "I can't be sure what Louise would have wanted and I'm trying to honor her wishes."

"She's dead, Evangeline. She doesn't have wishes anymore."

I did not want to get into a long conversation about Rayanne or the desires of Louise. I did not want her mixed in with us. We, the four of us—myself, Gabriel, Louise, and the house—we were separate from Rayanne, from everyone, and I wanted to keep us that way.

Rayanne had so many things going for her that I could not understand why she wanted the one thing I had, which was Gabriel. She was elegant and tall, with perfect clothes that she knew just how to wear. She was all rock 'n' roll beauty and edge, while I wasn't anything in particular. I had the same long, straight hair as she did and I wore clothes that looked like hers, but the result was not the same. I was missing that thing, whatever it was, that made certain people stand out. I was invisible most of the time while Rayanne was always visible.

When it was just Gabriel and me it was so easy. I didn't have to try. I didn't have to think about what I looked like. I preferred it that way. I knew it wasn't the way life worked, but I wished it could be for just a little while longer. Louise died, after all, and I inherited a house and it came with Gabriel inside of it to keep me company after she was gone. He was better than jewelry, or books, or money, or any of the usual things people receive when someone they love has passed away. It would be unfair of me not to fight for what Louise left me. In a way Rayanne was contesting Louise's will, and I was going to fight like hell to keep it from changing.

16

I maintained my belief that Gabriel and I were somehow fated, and I went with that instead of the more daunting possibility that he and Rayanne were more than friends.

We continued on as always, going from room to room and drawer to drawer, unraveling the life of Louise. The only room I avoided out of deference to her old, living self, was the workroom.

I was of course fascinated by the hours of unknown labor that took place behind that door. Labors which had absorbed Louise night after night until the sun rose for as many years as I could remember. My curiosity was a nagging, endless desire that I had literally been brought up with. Turning the doorknob would be like opening a present that had sat in front of me, perfectly wrapped, for my entire life. There was something beautiful about the idea of opening it, but something equally lovely about keeping it closed.

During the weeks that Gabriel had been coming to the Stone Crow, he too began to develop a strong interest in the contents of the room. He wondered, mainly from a scientific perspective, what types of things could have gone on in there hidden from the eyes of everyone for so many years.

It was the room itself that cemented Gabriel and me. By staying out of it I kept him, with his growing curiosity, by my side.

Day by day we moved through the house like figures in a dream, as though we were influencing each other's will. But there came a day when our synchronicity came to a stop in front of the door to the workroom. It was there that our oneness parted ways. His intense need to open the door butted up against my faithfulness to my grandmother. We stood in the chilly spot in the hallway.

"Open it," he said.

"I made a pact with her. It's unbreakable," I said, wrapping my arms around my ribs not for warmth but to protect myself against my desire to please him.

"She's dead."

"Do you need to keep saying that?"

"Apparently."

"Do you think her wishes should be ignored because she died?"

"That's just it, Evangeline, she doesn't have pacts or wishes any-more. Those things have a shelf life called death."

"I don't believe they disappear just because her body is gone."

"I do."

"You don't know what Louise wants in her death. With all the knowledge in the world, you still can't know if someone is able to want something after they die."

"So you're going to live in this house, you're going to sleep and eat here every day, and you're never going to open that door, not even out of normal, human curiosity, which Louise would still want you to possess, I'm sure."

"I'm *not* sure."

"Evangeline, you can tear your hair out over what your grand-mother's death means, what death means, period, or you can enjoy life, and get it over with and go inside. Think about it this way, whatever she did in there was really important to her. Do you think she'd want it to go unnoticed, undiscovered, lost forever?"

17

I had imagined complicated locks and combinations, something far more difficult than the turning of a knob. But the door opened eas-ily. And I was surprised at the simplicity. Apparently the only thing that had kept me out all of those years was the force of the look in Louise's eyes.

Inside was a short hallway that smelled of jasmine and flames, sweet and fiery. It smelled like Louise, only now, since her death, the scent was subtle, like dried flowers and logs burned long ago still sitting in a fireplace.

The essence of her, no matter how faint, was something I did not expect, and I momentarily lost my nerve. I stood still, breathing her in until Gabriel put his hand on my waist. It was the first time he had touched me and it startled me out of my sadness. His touch was confusing. It brought us closer, but took me away from Louise, so it became something I liked and didn't like at the same time.

On either side of the hallway were floor-to-ceiling shelves carved into stone walls and packed with vials and jars and decanters filled with liquids of every hue and possibility. It was cold and dark except for a little bit of light coming from underneath a door at the other end of the hall. The ray of light made the amber and red bottles glow like an ancient fire, while the cavelike stone walls made the daytime seem like the middle of the night in another century. It was as if the hallway had been left over from an earlier time, before the house had been built. As if the house had been built around it—a fortress created to hold its secrets. As we reached the door on the other side, the door to the white room, I pushed away my promise, the one I'd made to Louise, and stepped inside.

18

The whiteness was blinding. The room was exactly as she said it would be—a circle of nothing. Large and round with white walls, a white ceiling, a white floor, and an emptiness so pronounced that "nothingness" would hardly begin to describe it. If I had gone in alone I would have turned and run for my life.

Sadness was already visible in Gabriel's eyes and I felt bad that I had not prepared him beforehand for the feeling inside of the room. As he closed the door behind him the sorrow in his eyes was replaced with a pained, withdrawn look that covered his entire face.

The room was conical, like a twister, wide and circular at the top, narrowing to a smaller floor where the two of us stood. There was a white ladder leaning against the wall. It led to a ledge near the ceiling that circled the room and appeared wide enough to walk on.

Like two zombies we reached for the ladder. We climbed to the top, Gabriel first, and began walking around the room in single file.

It was hard to get our bearings in a space so white. It was disorienting in the extreme. There were no features, no textures, no way of knowing if we had walked ten steps or one, so we balanced as best we could on the ledge, sliding our fingertips along the smooth surface of the wall behind us like first-time ice-skaters gripping the railing.

It seemed to both of us that moving quickly was the best way to avoid falling away from the wall and onto the floor below.

"It's like a centrifuge," said Gabriel. "A machine that spins blood, breaking it up into its separate parts. The speed keeps the liquid pressed to the outside edges."

He stopped and leaned his back flat against the wall with his arms spread out like wings and his eyes closed. I closed mine too and forced pictures of grass and houses and people into my mind—anything to avoid the whiteness and the height.

I could hear the drip, drip, dripping of sweat running off Gabriel's face like water from a leaky faucet, each drop hitting the floor below and echoing through the room like a pebble in a canyon.

"Let's keep moving," I said, hoping that motion would stop the drops from falling off his face.

Round the room we went, sticking close to the wall until we found ourselves back at the ladder. We climbed down quickly and were going to leave the room as fast as we could, but there at the bottom of the ladder was something we had not seen at first. It was a low white table, small and square, and sitting on top of it was a much smaller white box.

The table was as white as the box, which was as white as the walls and the ceiling and the floor, which was probably why we missed it in the first place.

19

We stood together on the small floor at the bottom of the room until there was nothing left to do but leave or open the box.

"Do you want me to do it?" Gabriel asked.

I shook my head. Whatever it was, whatever it contained, I knew that it was between Louise and me.

I reached out an arm and lifted the lid, flicked it off with my fingertips, keeping my body as far away as possible. With the top gone we moved in closer and stared at the delicate object inside.

It was a small glass vial shaped like a teardrop, the color of a ruby. A tiny hole at the top of the tear held a crystal stopper, thin as a human hair. A single sheet of paper folded in half had my name, Evangeline, written in Louise's heavily slanted script.

"She knew you would end up in here," whispered Gabriel. "She knew you would break your promise."

My mouth felt dry. I licked my lips and picked up the note with shaky hands. As I unfolded the paper a brown spider, hairy and evil looking, fell onto the table. Its long legs slid down the side and disappeared underneath. I wasn't one for omens and signs of the future, but even I knew it wasn't a good one.

I unfolded the paper and read the note out loud:

Don't remove the crystal stopper, Evangeline,

unless you want everything in your life to change.

I leaned over the vial. It was then that I had a memory so vague, so distant, as not to be a memory at all, but more like a flashbulb illuminating a scene for just one second. Capturing a vision like that was difficult. Miss a beat, think another thought, and it's gone forever.

Louise and I were in her bedroom and it was a very long time ago, the year I had cut my forehead sleepwalking in the middle of the night.

"How does your skin smell?" she asked me.

I lifted my arm to my nose and smiled.

"Not even the great perfumeries in the South of France can make something like that," she said. "Not Hermès, nor Guerlain, nor even Chanel can re-create the scent of childhood."

And then she held up the vial and said the same words as appeared in the note: "Do not remove the stopper, Evangeline, unless you want everything in your life to change."

I loved my grandmother and the Stone Crow and I could not see any reason to want to change anything, ever, and during the years in between then and now I had forgotten all about the tiny glass teardrop filled with the strange, life-changing liquid.

Carefully, I picked up the ruby vial. It was warm, almost hot to the touch, as if something alive were inside. I handed it to Gabriel and I saw the veins in his hand jump at the contact. He placed it back in the box. Sometimes things happen that cement people together forever because they occur in secrecy, when no one else is around. This was one of those times and we both knew it.

I stared down at the vial, straight through the liquid to the stopper, thin as a human hair, the only thing that held back what would change me, and possibly us, for the rest of our lives.

It was hard to know what to do. Gabriel's life was going well and I couldn't imagine that he wanted anything more. He was in medical school and he was on his way, so to speak, to the good life. I, on the other hand, was still lacking any discernable direction. Change wouldn't, or at least shouldn't, be as difficult for me.

But in the end it was Gabriel.

"Don't you want to know what it is?" he asked. "What it's made of, what it feels like, what it smells like, and what it does? How many people get a chance at a whole new life right in the middle of the one they have?"

But I couldn't do it for him. I had to think about whether I wanted to change and what it meant. Would it be physical or would I be different on the inside only? Would I be able to go back to the way I was if I wanted to?

"Let's go to the park and sit in the grass and look at the sky," he said. "It's the room that's making us think like this."

"Like what?"

"Like this is a real possibility."

"If Louise says everything will change, it will."

"Think about me," said Gabriel. "How awful it would be to go through my life without knowing what's inside. I would never be able to concentrate on anything else. I would have to try and forget about this day, and that would be sad and impossible and I might never graduate from medical school, or fall in love, not fully anyway, because all I'd be thinking about is this little red piece of glass."

"It's all I have left of Louise," I said. "I'm afraid if I open it, she'll be gone."

"You have the house, and this room and all the times you had together and all the things she told you over all the summers you spent here," said Gabriel. "You have so much more of her than that liquid. You have memories."

But the tiny vial *was* her. It was everything she worked toward and everything she loved. And every single thing I've done since I walked into her house years ago has led me straight to it. It was the culmination of Louise herself.

"She knew you would get me into this room somehow," I said in a low voice. "That was your only job, that was your purpose here today. It's why she left you to me."

"Stop saying that; it's creepy and it's not true. I barely knew her."

Gabriel and I left the white room behind, backing out of it, not taking our eyes off it, as if neither of us could believe it was there in the first place.

⌇

I lay down on my back on Louise's bed, with my feet on the floor, holding the vial to my chest. Gabriel collapsed right next to me, hard. The mattress bounced up and down and vibrated before settling into place. It was not how I'd imagined our first time in bed, but there we were.

"Louise is dead but you have *me*," he said.

"I know, but it's not the same. You're you and nobody else could ever be you. But nobody else could ever be her either."

From what I could tell, Gabriel came from one of those families where the sons become doctors, lawyers, teachers. He came from a supportive family. There was no way he could understand what Louise was to someone who came from a family like mine.

⌇

I must have been tired, because walking was an effort, like moving through sand, but I got up off the bed and leaned the vial against the mirror that sat on the mantel over the fireplace. Its reflection made two vials, twice the amount of change. I crawled back through the sand and lay down next to Gabriel. We stayed like that, not touching and not talking, like two people who have lived together for a long, long time.

20

We slept side by side on the bed with our feet on the floor through-
out the night. I don't think either of us moved an inch, and if we
hadn't been woken up by the banging on the front door we probably could have gone on and on, like marathon sleepers, for the
next twenty-six hours.

"I brought lunch," said Rayanne, standing in the doorway in her
fantastic rock-star clothes: a short vintage fur over a silver tank top
and skin-tight jeans showing off pointy hip bones and tucked into
worn-out leather boots. She looked so good that I couldn't help
feeling attracted to her in a way I didn't in real life, but I might
toward a girl in a dream.

I looked down and touched my body to make sure I wasn't
asleep. I was awake but I was still in yesterday's wrinkled clothes
with unbrushed teeth, uncombed hair, and no shoes. I could feel
myself shrinking next to Rayanne, actually becoming physically
smaller, which happened whenever I felt overpowered by someone
else's intelligence or beauty.

Rayanne brought two things with her this time around, as if she
herself were not enough for me to deal with. Slung over her shoulder was a plastic bag full of food, and at her side was a tall, skinny,
sullen-looking boy with skin-tight black jeans, black work boots, a
white T-shirt, and long black hair that completely covered his left
eye like a patch.

Gabriel and I were inside the doorway while they stood on the
stone porch, on the other side. I didn't invite them in because I could
not help feeling that there was an invisible wall between us—a thin,
clear, cellophane barrier that could not be bridged. They were on
the outside and we were on the inside like two different worlds just
inches apart, separated by a membrane that only I could see. Separated by the knowledge of the white room and the ruby red vial.

"Did you just wake up?" asked Rayanne without a trace of
jealousy.

"We were fast asleep," said Gabriel.

"Together?" asked Rayanne with a teasing toss of her hair and a laugh, as if she knew with complete certainty that the answer was no.

Gabriel reached across the invisible barrier and took her hand. I could hear the cellophane tear. It was loud, as if it were happening right against my eardrum, and I was surprised at how easily his hand went through.

I cringed, hopefully just on the inside.

"This is Paul," Rayanne said to me, holding her free hand out toward him as if she were presenting me with a gift. As if she were saying, Gabriel is mine, but don't feel too bad, you can have this instead.

The sullen boy said hello by pushing his hair out of his eye with a sweep of his right hand across his forehead. I stared at the newly uncovered eye. I had expected it to be a different color than the other one, or simply not there at all.

The four of us walked to the center of town. Cyril was so small that the cemetery doubled as a park, with gravestones right next to picnic tables and barbecue pits. The lawn was low and always perfectly cut out of respect for the dead, and when the sun peeked out from behind a cloud the grass took on a fake-looking bright green, as if it were crop-dusted with spray paint. Rayanne sat next to Gabriel without a second thought, as if that was where she belonged. He leaned his back against *Mrs. Mae Forrester, beloved wife of John Forrester,* 1920–1997. I sat across from them next to sullen boy, propped up by *Stephen Raymond Anderson,* 1958–2006.

Neither Gabriel nor I mentioned the workroom or the vial. Those things belonged to the dark, inside world of the house, while the lunch belonged to the bright, outside world of Cyril. The barrier between the two worlds was dense, and sitting in the park, on one side of it, I almost felt like I could forget the challenge of the vial—that's how I'd started to look at it, like a challenge to change.

Sullen boy asked me if I wanted a sandwich, but I couldn't eat.

"Her grandmother just died," said Rayanne.

It was an excuse, Louise's death, when really I couldn't eat because I was fixated on Gabriel's arm, which was too close to Rayanne's, one point of his perfect star birthmark almost touching the skin on her elbow, the space between them thin as a leaf.

"At least have some coffee," she said.

She passed me a thermos from inside her bag, another mini inside world.

"Do you mind if I drink from here?"

"Go ahead."

I unscrewed the lid and drank from the bottle. The coffee was so hot I had an instant blister on the roof of my mouth.

I got a little hungrier when I noticed Gabriel looking at me. At this point he had his arm around Rayanne, but his eyes were definitely on me. He looked like a person split in two, as if I had his head and his thoughts, and Rayanne had his body. She had the better part of the deal as far as I was concerned.

"So, Evangeline, are you going to stay here?" she asked, pulling a beer out of the bag. "I mean from now on?"

She looked slightly more intimidating, if that was possible, with the beer in her hand.

"Yes," I said in a calm voice. "I am."

"Good," she said in a not very convincing one.

"Rayanne's going to medical school in a few years," said Gabriel.

"Slow down," she said, shoving him softly. "I've got to get through undergrad first."

Great. I had a blister the size of a silver dollar threatening to gush in my mouth, and Rayanne was touching Gabriel's arm and going to medical school.

"What are you going to do?" I asked sullen boy.

"I'm going to play guitar."

Of course you are, I thought.

"There's a party Saturday night," said Gabriel to me. "Paul's playing. Why don't you come?"

I saw Rayanne look at him and frown slightly, almost imperceptibly, unless you were a person like me who watched every single interaction between them as if they were cells under a microscope and you were a cancer researcher.

I didn't answer right away because I didn't know if my heart could take a night of watching the two of them holding hands, or worse, but of course I already knew I was going. I knew I did not have the willpower to pass up an evening with the opportunity to be near Gabriel even if he chose to be near someone else.

The four of us walked out of the cemetery together.

"See ya, Crab," sullen boy said to Rayanne.

"Crab?"

"It's my name. Rayanne Crabbe, with a double b and an e at the end. So what?"

"Pull in your pincers, Rayanne," said Gabriel, opening and closing the four fingers of both hands against his thumbs.

Rayanne's last name being Crabbe was the first piece of good news I had heard in a long time, and as she and Gabriel walked away I could swear she was moving sideways.

༄

I indulged myself in the pain of watching the two of them walk down Main Street. As if the lunch in the graveyard wasn't clear enough, as if I didn't already know the truth, I searched for even more signs of their togetherness, and of course I found them: handholding, arms touching, faces turning toward each other with staring eyes and smiling mouths—I did not even need to hear the words.

I watched until the last possible second, when they were nothing more than tiny dots in my vision. I saw everything in their long walk, and trying to hide it from my mind was futile.

Watching them disappear on the horizon I thought about the glass vial and the possibility of changing everything in my life. Maybe I could change Gabriel into my boyfriend, instead of Rayanne's. Maybe the ruby liquid would make him feel about me the way he felt about her. Maybe Louise had invented the antidote to loneliness.

21

The afternoon sun tired me, and when I got back to the Stone Crow I took the vial off the mantelpiece, lay down on my bed, fell asleep immediately, and dreamed of Louise. Her beehive came into my mind first, then her blue eyes, and finally her sweet lips, thin but never stern, which said words, which I hoped even from the confines of my dream I would not forget upon awakening or ever after.

"Change can be sudden, or slow, like a dream,
It can rip out your heart or bring you peace,
But it can never stop being what it is, Evangeline,
Which is something that never stops being.
In other words,
In the battle between holding on and letting go
Change will win, every time."

I opened my eyes and grabbed a pen and paper off the nightstand and wrote, knowing that to forget would be a mistake, and then I sank back into a deep sleep.

Hours later when I woke up and reread her words, tears came into my eyes. They weren't tears of despair at the fact that she was no longer here, they were the kind that come when something happens that's not sad or happy, but surprising, creepy, or simply not understandable. They were tears for the things that jolt the mind.

When Gabriel came over the next morning, I gave him the pad to read. When he was done he covered his mouth with the palm of his hand and spread his fingers across his face from the top of the cheekbone to the jawline. His hand placement had the same feeling as my tears. Shock. Surprise. Jolt. I knew that he understood.

"In the battle between holding on and letting go, change will win, every time," he said. "It's a mistake to try to keep things the way they are. It's not even possible," he said. "That's what she means."

The two of us turned toward the vial on the mantel at the same moment, like lost synchronized swimmers trying to stay in formation. We stared at the tiny glass bottle of inevitability.

"Are you ready now?" he asked.

"I am," I said.

22

I held the vial in my hand and gazed at its ruby red color so full of the promise of change, of Gabriel being mine instead of Rayanne's, and of life having a happy ending. I knew all about fairy tales never coming true, about men leaving the women who love them in the middle of the night, and mothers and daughters divided, but I wasn't so far gone that I lacked all hope, so, slowly, ever so slowly, I pulled on the crystal stopper, sliding it toward me until it was all the way out of the vial.

A mist rose up so fast it was as if it had been pressing up against the tiny glass, waiting forever to be released. I could see it in the air and I put my face into its gray dampness and breathed the liquid fog into my body, first through my nose and then as deep inside of my lungs as I could.

It had a strange scent, dual in nature. It was dark, like death by fire, and very light, like sunshine and freedom. I felt as if I could choose the side I wanted to be on. As if the perfume were asking me: *Evangeline, are you darkness or are you light?*

I put the stopper itself to my nose. The power of it made me sit down on my dead grandmother's bed. Straight from the vial, the layers were less abstract, and more distinct. There was jasmine from the south of India, and red velvet roses molting on the vine. Further down there was the unmistakable scent of leather warmed by a slow-burning fire.

But still, there was something else in the perfume that I could not name. I inhaled many times in an attempt to understand it, and although I couldn't I knew without a doubt that it was the most important ingredient in the vial. If I had to describe it, I'd say it was the scent of darkness.

I replaced the stopper, which because of its thinness and the tiny hole it needed to fill, was like threading a needle, and put the vial back on the mantel.

❧

Gabriel, who had been watching from the bed, came over and stood in front of me. He took the strands of hair that had fallen onto my face and hooked them behind my ears. He didn't say a word but he took the vial off the mantel and handed it back to me.

"You have to," he said. "Louise told you so in your dream. She's waiting for you to put her life's work onto your body, Evangeline."

At first I thought I still had a choice. But then I realized that everything Gabriel and I had been through from the moment we met was like a dream, and the one thing about dreams is that there are no choices. We dream what we dream. It's a choiceless world we live in, in the middle of the night.

I took the vial from him and put it against the veins of my wrist. It felt warm. I lifted out the stopper for the second time, took a deep breath, and before I could think too hard about dreams and freedom of choice I tipped the tiny piece of glass back against my neck. I heard a slight sizzle when the liquid touched my skin and for just a second it felt like ants burrowing.

I put it against my skin a second time, but there was only one drop left inside, one last bit of change. The small amount made me less afraid. After all, how much could I change from just one drop?

23

Gabriel took my arm and brought me over to the mirror on the other side of the room where the light was better. The scent had left a red mark on my neck like a boy had been sucking there.

He put his finger on the mark.

"Does it hurt?"

It didn't, but I felt the liquid inside of me as if I'd drunk it down instead of putting it on my skin. Warmth spread through my limbs like the poison might from a scorpion's tail, branching and branching until it was trapped against the edges of my body, pooling in my fingertips and my toes, with nowhere left to go.

As the moments passed a definite scent came up through my pores. It began slowly. First from the inside of my arms, and then from my palms. It rose from my legs and then my thighs and then my breasts. Yes. It was coming from everywhere. Fire and jasmine, leather and rose. I was a repository for Louise's life's work, alive, and inside of me.

"Can you smell it?" I asked Gabriel.

He put his face so close to my body I could feel the moisture from his breath.

"I can."

Gabriel and I faced each other on the bed. We sat there for hours. I had no idea either of us possessed that kind of patience. Slow as time the scent ripened and deepened, growing more remote and strange with each passing minute. Hot and dark and sweet, my fragrance was as mesmerizing as looking up and seeing a fire on the moon.

It was not like any type of perfume that I knew but like nature itself, organically beautiful, as if the scent had been made from the inside of my body and hadn't come from the vial at all. As if it had been sitting inside me for years, a wine that had finally found its perfect moment.

Gabriel breathed in this new part of me. He seemed unfocused and unable to stand up or let go of my hands.

"What's it like for you?" I asked him.

He leaned closer, closed his eyes and inhaled.

"Like sweetness," he said, "with a little bit of poison that makes the sweetness, sweeter."

The scent from my body was like a third person, a beautiful person that both of us fell in love with right away. I wanted to free it from the confines of my clothes, to give it expression and let it loose into the room and into Gabriel's body.

I took off my T-shirt and laid it on the edge of the bed and Gabriel leaned forward and pressed his face against my chest. I could feel his long eyelashes on my collarbone. I stood up in front of him and took off my jeans and he did the same.

"The scent is coming from the inside of your mouth," he said. "From the air coming out of your lungs. From your tongue and your lips."

I pushed down on his shoulders and laid my body on top of his. We weren't friends anymore.

Change.

24

We stayed inside for three days. Gabriel showered after each time we were together, but I didn't because I was afraid the scent would wash off and I wasn't naïve or vain enough to think it was just me that he wanted. Something beautiful had come from the union of my angel Gabriel and me, and I didn't want to go back to the way we were before. If the scent were to wear off there was the chance he might wake up out of the stupor of sex and try to do the right thing by Rayanne, whatever that was. Being Gabriel, I was sure his moral compass was still intact. I was in love, which meant that mine was already gone.

I feared that he was someone who could leave me and not look back, while I was someone who clung on to things for years when everyone else around me had long forgotten that they'd ever taken place. I hated that about myself—that my mind could never let go of anything. I knew I'd cling to the memory of Gabriel forever. I knew I'd be a hundred before I loved anyone else. And I knew I could not let that happen.

As I lay in bed thinking of how he would leave if I lost the beauty of the scent, he took my hand, pulled me toward the bathroom. Still holding my hand he turned on the water in the shower and let it run until the temperature was inviting.

"We have the party to go to tonight. Remember? With Rayanne and Paul."

I wondered how he could think about the outside world at a time like this.

"Paul's band is playing," he said.

I could feel him slipping away with every word. Each time he opened his mouth it was as if I could see him sliding backward and away.

"I remember," I said, "but I'd rather stay here. Wouldn't you?"

"Either way you have to take a shower, Evangeline."

"I don't want to."

"It's not healthy. People get sick this way. I read about it all the time in school. Whole populations die off just from being dirty."

I couldn't have cared less about getting sick or being filthy. I had someone of my own who wanted to love me day and night.

"It could wash down the drain and be gone forever," I said, "and there isn't any more left. Can we risk that?"

He put his hands on my shoulders and tucked the loose strands of my hair behind my ears the way he did when he wanted to make a point, as if it were possible that I could hear him better that way.

"You need to get into the water, Eva. If you don't the scent will be gone soon anyway, overpowered by the smell of your own body, and it won't be good. Believe me, baby."

I repeated that sentence over and over in my mind, holding on to the last three words only, the ones where he called me his baby.

"Think about it this way," he said, "if you take a shower and it goes away, we'll always have these three nights. It's almost more perfect this way."

He had casually crystallized all of my fears into one sentence, and I tried very hard to remember that he was not a cruel person by nature.

I stood in the bathroom with one foot on the side of the tub as if it were a crossroads. I stared at the showerhead as if there were fire rushing out of it instead of water, as if it were capable of ruining everything that was beautiful about me.

"You're not going to stay with me if the scent goes away, are you?" I asked, not looking at him but watching the drops of water hitting the walls around the tub.

"I'll still be here with you, Evangeline," he said to the back of my head. "We'll sit around sometime in the future when we're both old and talk about the time when you were . . . like this."

"Louise told me that scent could make you love someone you might not even like. How can you be sure how you feel about me?"

"I wanted you in the park, before any of this happened."

"Why didn't you say it then?"

"I was with Rayanne. The time wasn't right."

I stepped into the shower, afraid and trying not to be, for fear that even strong emotions could ruin the scent. There were probably so many things that could do it. I just didn't know what they were yet and small things seemed suddenly treacherous.

I ran a loofah, without soap, across my back and legs. The water going down the drain was brown and dirty. Gabriel sat down on the side of the tub and took off his shirt. He put an arm around both of my legs and pressed his face against the side of my thigh. With his free hand he washed my feet. I watched the water run over his blue star birthmark, then I turned my body toward him, closed my eyes, and pressed myself against his face.

I loved the way Gabriel and I had sex. We didn't have words and promises, breakups and breakdowns. We just had this strange adventure we'd somehow gotten involved in together.

I wrapped my hair in a towel and he dried my body with another.

"What are you going to tell Rayanne?" I asked.

"I don't know. She's a good person and I don't want to hurt her," but he was already pulling the towel off my hair and burying his face in the scented strands.

Fire and leather, jasmine and rose, it was still there on my body and in my hair. If anything the scent was even stronger, coming off my warm, damp skin.

It wasn't going to wash off in the shower. It wasn't going to go away. It was part of me now, like eye color or shoe size.

Gabriel carried me back to the bedroom with his head still in my hair and my knees draped over his forearms.

"What's the scent like, for you?" he asked.

"It's like being covered in magic," I said.

25

We walked through the empty nighttime streets of Cyril holding hands, moving fast, heading straight toward the party and Rayanne, the one person with any potential to take Gabriel away from me.

I had on tight, faded jeans, brown cowboy boots, and a V-neck T-shirt worn so thin it was almost see-through, but not quite. My hope was that the shirt would help tip the scales in my favor in case, in the face of Rayanne, the scent did not.

Gabriel wore black jeans with a hole in the knee and a black T-shirt. He looked a bit tougher than usual, which made me think that he was gearing up for an argument with Rayanne, mentally preparing himself through the choice of his clothing.

The moon was low and full but it was a foggy night so nothing was clear. From the outside we could hear Paul's guitar and someone keeping rhythm on the drums. There was a squat, tough-looking man standing in front of the door. He had faded red and gray hair, and a long, coarse beard. He wore motorcycle boots and jeans with a heavy chain around his hips. He looked us up and down, his eyes landing on my worn out V-neck, and waved us in.

The house was packed with people creating a heat that must have been somewhere up around ninety degrees. The walls were painted matte black and the lamps had dark red bulbs, giving the room a cavelike feel, but hot instead of cool. I looked at Gabriel and saw a drop of sweat slide into his ear. Another drop followed it, hanging off his lobe like a silver earring. Hit with the smell of smoke and alcohol we stood still, trying to adjust after the days spent in bed at the Stone Crow, but then we stopped fighting it, and walked into the crowd.

"Who lives here?" I shouted.

"No one," said Gabriel. "There was a fire two years ago. The family left. They didn't come back, and the house was never repaired."

We moved through a wall of people to get closer to the band.

"In Louisiana they call this devil music," said Gabriel.

"What?" I yelled.

"Devil music. They say the steady, rhythmic sound of the drums conjures up evil spirits."

"Like Rayanne?" I asked, feeling bad as soon as the words were out of my mouth.

Gabriel threw his head back and showed a mouthful of teeth like he was laughing, or angry. I couldn't tell which because I couldn't hear him, but I wouldn't have blamed him if he was mad. I wanted him so badly that Rayanne had become an evil spirit in my mind, but I knew she was simply the girl who got to him before I did.

He took my hand in the darkness and we pushed through smoke and bodies until we were right up in front of the music. There was a girl with dark, side-swept bangs in a long, dirty rabbit vest singing a song about a house made of bones. The fur made her look like a rabid dog as she sang into the mike and I wondered how she could stand the heat.

Paul's guitar made an eerie sound behind her and Gabriel started dancing with one hand holding a beer bottle and his shiny hair falling over his face.

I must have looked surprised.

"Two years in Louisiana," he said.

We danced in privacy—everyone else in the room disappeared from our minds. It was easy to accomplish. A carryover from our days alone in bed.

Gabriel finished his beer and rolled the empty bottle on the floor. He held my hips, moving me in to him with his hands, keeping his eyes closed and his nose and mouth buried in my hair, the same as he had been in the bathroom with his face between my legs. There was no longer any separation between Gabriel and my scent. I knew there was nothing that could keep him away.

I brushed his hair behind his ears and felt the sweat on his forehead.

"You're something to see," I said.

I rested my chin on his shoulder and pressed my body into his and for a long time I danced like that with my eyes closed, but when I opened them I saw that we were not alone at all, but completely surrounded.

My first thought was that they were there for Gabriel, as attracted as I was to his shiny black hair, narrow hips, and blue star, but then I felt a new pair of hands on my waist. I looked over my shoulder and saw the man with the long beard from the front door.

"What are you doing?" I yelled.

"I'm dancing with you," he said in an even tone.

"I don't know you," I said, trying to move away but not finding anywhere to go in the crush of people.

"Don't matter, sweetie, it's a party."

I looked Gabriel in the eye and he bent down and picked up his beer bottle from the floor. He held it up for the man to see.

"Walk away," he said.

"Are you threatening me?" said the man, his mouth a dark circle, his lips barely visible under the mustache and beard.

Gabriel stepped in front of me and held the neck of the bottle tight in his fist.

"I wouldn't do that if I were you," said the man. "There's a world of people right behind me and all they want to do is touch your girlfriend. I'm the only thing stopping them right now. The only thing standing between them and her."

Gabriel held the bottle tight.

"Have it your way, boy," he said. "I'm just the hired help."

He backed up a few steps and then turned around and pushed his way through the crowd toward the front door. Although he was a large man, the space he left was filled in an instant.

I felt on edge. There was no air and no space in the room and the heat was making the scent of my skin gain power. Many bodies crowded around us until Gabriel and I were dead center in a vortex of people as if the party had turned into some strange spiral pattern with us as the bull's-eye.

"What are you wearing?" asked a girl with teardrops tattooed under her eye.

"She smells like love," a guy shouted, his diamond earrings and short blond hair glinting in the blue light of his cigarette.

People were pushing and fighting to get closer. I was confused. Up until that moment I had allowed myself to imagine that Gabriel and I were the only ones who could smell Louise's perfume, but now it was clear that its effect was more far-reaching than either of us had thought.

"That's some potent shit," someone breathed into my ear.

Gabriel grabbed my arm and pulled me through the crowd while people shoved their noses at me like I was a dog in the park.

I spotted a tiny drop of moonlight coming in through the mailbox slat in the front door and I trained my eyes on it, blocking out everything else, and using it as a point of focus, a kind of saving grace, as we pushed through the crowd.

We were almost free when Rayanne put her hands on Gabriel's back.

"Where are you going?" she asked. "I just got here."

I looked back and I could see a wall of people moving toward us.

"We have to go," I said.

She turned and saw the bodies moving in our direction.

"Come on," said Gabriel.

We reached the front door and pulled it open. The three of us ran down the street, around the corner, and onto the lawn of a house with no lights. We bent down between two weeping willow trees with our hands on our knees to catch our breath. I could hear the party spilling out onto the street behind us and I hoped that the long strands of hairlike branches from the willow tree would hide us from sight.

"Let's go into the backyard," said Gabriel. "It's safer."

As soon as we started walking along the side of the house two spotlights went on and we ran into the garden of the neighboring house instead.

"Jesus," said Rayanne, "are you kidding me? What is going on?"

"Stand still," I said. "Don't say a word and just breathe."

"What are you talking about?"

"Put your face up to Evangeline's neck," said Gabriel.

"What?"

"Just do it."

Rayanne looked at Gabriel through squinted eyes of confusion as Gabriel pulled my hair back. She leaned in toward me.

"I don't see anything," she said. "What am I looking for?"

The scent was not nearly as strong outside as it had been in the dense, unbearable heat of the party, so I asked her to move in closer.

She was so near to me that her nose was pressed up against my thumping jugular vein.

"Wow," she said, and moved away from me suddenly, as if she'd been blown back by a strong wind.

She turned to Gabriel.

"Is this why you've been helping her clean her house?"

I watched him intently.

He shook his head no.

"She wasn't like this when I met her."

Rayanne leaned in to me a second time, against her will, I could tell. Her nose lingered at my collarbone for a moment and this time I could feel her lips brush against me. Her tongue touched the red mark on my neck. I let her do it. I knew she had no choice.

She straightened up and looked at Gabriel and me with her mouth still open, her teeth glowing white in the moonlight, and then she turned her back and walked away.

It was as if all at once, in an overwhelming moment of intuition, she knew that she had no chance. That no skinny body in vintage clothes, or long straight hair was going to bring him back. No words were going to work either—they were not any competition for what I had become, or rather, for what was coming out of me.

I felt bad for Rayanne and bad for myself too. I didn't win Gabriel's love fairly, through the force of my personality, or the power of my own love. I'd won him over because of a potion my dead grandmother left for me in a red teardrop. How could I explain that to Rayanne, or to anyone else at all?

I watched Gabriel watch her walk away. He did not make one small step, not a single, placating, false start in her direction and I wondered if I had stolen him from his true destiny. If I had somehow moved him and Rayanne off their natural course.

He took my hand and we walked back to Louise's house where

we belonged. We didn't say anything. We both knew the reason we were together was unnatural and unbreakable.

26

"It isn't just you and me anymore," Gabriel said. "Everyone is attracted to you now."

He took pots out of the drawers underneath the kitchen sink and set them on the stove. He did not look my way and he seemed distant, almost angry at what life had placed in front of him, namely me.

"Are you upset about Rayanne? Do you miss her?"

"No," he said. "You've already managed to erase her from my heart and I don't feel good about it but it's the truth. I'm not mad, I'm just trying to keep my hands busy so I can have a conversation with you without touching you."

I stepped back toward the opposite side of the room.

"What are you making?"

"It doesn't matter. I'm only cooking so that I can smell something besides you."

There was that edge in his voice again.

He turned up the fire and poured oil into a skillet and water into a pot and then he lined up the jars of spice that Louise kept on the countertop: parsley, oregano, bay leaves, pepper, and thyme, and mini branches of herbs, including basil and dill as well as some lemons and fresh cloves of garlic. He added them to the oil. His plan worked—the kitchen filled up with new odors that did not quite overcome my own, but were certainly gaining ground.

"The ancient Romans wore bay leaves on their heads for virility," he said.

"You don't need any," I said.

"Borage is used to induce abortion. We learned that in the first year of med school."

"I don't need any."

"Arabs believe that cardamom builds good feelings among friends."

"We don't need any other people in our lives."

"I'm showing off, you know."

"I know. Keep going."

"Let's see. Curry powder should always be browned in butter. Fenugreek is hairy and it'll make you dream of sex. Ginger makes men horny, but not women. Lavender should be spread on the bedsheets. Not yours, of course, we don't need to add any more scent to your bed, but it can also be used in making soup."

"I'm impressed."

Gabriel opened the refrigerator and pulled out whatever he could find. He sliced through red peppers, onions, and garlic with more power than was necessary. He cut the tips off asparagus spears with the phenomenal dexterity of someone who could become a surgeon. He tossed the vegetables into the hot skillet, stirring with one hand while pulling a box of spaghetti out of the cabinet with the other.

He grabbed some sausage from the refrigerator that I hadn't even noticed and that may have been there since Louise, sliced through it with a meat cleaver, and tossed it in with the vegetables. He added the herbs and spices and then wiped his fragrant hands on a dish towel.

"The final touch," he said, "is brandy. It's my own little trick. It brings out the best in the meat." He pulled a small, airline-size bottle out of his pocket.

"I bought this for the party, but it's better used in here."

I liked watching Gabriel cook. Lifting the iron pots made the muscles of his arms more prominent and the intense, focused look of his eyes on something other than me gave me the freedom to watch him without feeling self-conscious. He wasn't smiling but he looked happier than he had at any other time that night.

I put my arms around his waist and breathed in the aroma of his hair and the food at the same time.

He turned around.

"I think I did it," he said. "I can smell the food clear as day, and I can't smell you at all."

It was irrational, I knew, but I was jealous of pasta with herbs and spices.

He came over to the table with a sprig of dill in his hand. He crushed the leaves between his fingers, held my arm down on the table and smeared it on my wrists, killing my scent even further. Then he strained the pasta, brought it to the table and placed it on a hot plate between us. He poured the vegetables and meat on top and handed me a fork. I could barely see him through the steam.

"I thought the scent of food might give me some space and freedom so I could understand how I feel about you. I don't want to make any mistakes, like I did with Rayanne."

"Mistakes about what?"

"About taking you to New Orleans. I want you to live with me for the fall semester. I'm thinking we can try it out and see what happens. I don't want to leave you here. I *can't* leave you here now."

"You're not responsible for what I've become."

"Come with me, Evangeline. I'm pretty sure I can't be without you."

"I don't know. Chicken bones, frizzly hens, all that voodoo stuff gives me the creeps."

He got up and put his arms around me.

"How do you know about frizzly hens?"

"I just do."

"Strange."

"Louise and Fayetteville."

"Ah, yes, Louise. Well, do I give you the creeps?"

"No."

"That's right. And besides, there's a lot more to New Orleans than that. There's gumbo and bread pudding and fried chicken. There are old Victorian homes, music everywhere, and the friendliest, nicest people anywhere."

"I'll drive you crazy with this scent. You won't get any work done."

"I don't know about that. You might be the only person on earth who can erase the smell of formaldehyde from the cadaver lab. Last year it stuck to me wherever I went, and made me dream about dead people all night long."

"Where would we stay?"

"I have a friend who has a place in the French Quarter. He's a painter and he could use the money."

"You never talk about him."

"I never needed his apartment."

"Let me think about it."

Gabriel picked me up and held me in his arms with his nose in my chest.

"You'll have more freedom there," he said. "New Orleans has a scent of its own that's strong almost all the time. Magnolia, sweet olive, jasmine, and chicory-flavored coffee. I doubt anyone will notice you there. Let me give you something beautiful and tender and delicate and tasty, like what you give me every day now, with your skin. Let me give you New Orleans."

꒰꒱

As the summer wore on and Gabriel and I planned for the fall semester I forgot all about the moment when I tipped the vial against my neck and felt the liquid crawl through my body. The line between the scent and my self blurred, and it became a part of me, as though my body possessed a kind of genius, like a high IQ, or a talent at math, a gift that was given to me at birth.

Realistically I knew that it was left to me in a bottle by my grandmother, but still, I smelled so dusky and deep, warm and unique, that it was hard not to feel like it was a special combination of Louise's talent and my body, that Louise's liquid, together with my own chemistry, was what made the scent so extraordinary, and because it came from my grandmother, it felt almost genetic. By summer's end I'd completely convinced myself that on another person, the vial might have had no effect at all. In fact, I began to believe that I was born with it.

27

"Hi, Mom."

"Evangeline, is that you?"

"Why do you ask things like that?" I said. "You know it's me."

"I haven't heard from you in so long I forgot what your voice sounds like."

"You have a phone too."

"How's everything going with the house? A lot of work, I suppose?"

"Everything's fine. The house is pretty much cleaned out."

"Have you decided what you're going to do with it?"

"What do you mean?"

"Are you going to put it up for sale?"

"Louise gave it to me, Mom. If she wanted me to sell it, she would have said, 'Sell the house, Evangeline.' I'm keeping it."

"Well, it's probably best that way. No one would buy that old place anyway."

"I called to tell you that I'm going to New Orleans for a while. I'll be gone for a few weeks, maybe a little longer."

There was a long silence on the phone. I could hear my mother's mind working, causing actual static in the airwaves.

"It's a boy, isn't it?" she said.

"Yes. I'm going with a boy I met up here."

"Are you pregnant, Evangeline?"

"No, I'm not pregnant!"

My mother believed that what happened to her would happen to every girl, everywhere, in exactly the same way.

"So you're going down south to party and waste your time with a boy from Cyril? What about college? Have you thought about it at all?"

I moved my mouth away from the phone and let out a deep breath in a way that she couldn't hear. The call had of course been a mistake.

"If you would let me talk I was just about to tell you that I'm going to look at Tulane and Louisiana State," I lied. "I'm thinking about applying for next year. I thought you'd want to know."

"Yes. I'd hate to come all the way up to that godforsaken town just to find you gone."

"You would never come up here, Mom. You didn't even come for Louise's funeral."

"I might have," she said. "But you went for me. It's one of the perks of having a child."

Whenever I was away from my mother for any length of time I had a fantasy that when we spoke to each other again we would be close. But when I got off the phone it occurred to me that my "flesh and blood" knew absolutely nothing about me. Not the slightest thing. If I had to guess I would bet she didn't even know the basics—my favorite color, ice-cream flavor, or subject at school.

Before hearing her voice I had played around with the idea of telling her about the vial and the workroom and Gabriel, but as we spoke I realized that telling her those things would be like walking up to a total stranger and discussing the most intimate details of my life.

28

It was pouring on and off the night before we left for New Orleans. I fell asleep in the quiet moments between the small storms and woke up gasping, my eyes burning as if I'd come up from the sea, each time the rain began. I don't believe in signs and messages from unknown sources, but I had to admit, at least to myself, that it wasn't a good start to the trip.

"It's pretty humid in New Orleans," Gabriel said, lying next to me. "It can rain for days on end. Are you going to be okay with that?"

"I'll get used to it," I said. "That's the key to things, you know— getting used to them."

"So the trip might be good for you, then?"

I faked a smile.

"The more rain the better."

There was no point in letting Gabriel witness the worst of my fears just when he was most in love. I got out of bed, went into Louise's bathroom, and took her leftover sleeping pills from the medicine cabinet. I took one for that night and put the rest in my suitcase for the first stormy night in New Orleans.

⌇

The next morning, refreshed from the sleeping pill, I went to say goodbye to Father Madrid. I walked down Main Street and over to the butcher shop, where he kept an apartment on the second floor. At one time he lived in the rectory next to the church but a fire had forced him to move out. When the rectory was rebuilt, he was already comfortable above the butcher shop and he didn't want to move back.

I was too young to remember the incident, but my mother believed it was arson. She suggested, through the tone of her voice, that Father Madrid had set the fire himself so that he could move into a new place where he would not have to share his rooms with other members of the clergy.

I didn't want to believe her, but it was true that he had lived dormitory style in the rectory while at the butcher shop he had his own apartment—kitchen, bathroom, living room, and bedroom all to himself. I was no fire-starter, but I could understand doing it in order to get my own space and not have to live in a small, single room with another human being all of the time.

At the butcher shop I climbed up the wooden stairs, which ran in a Z formation along the outside wall, and pressed the button marked *Fr. Madrid.* I had my mouth close to the intercom all ready with my speech about why I was at his apartment when he buzzed me in without asking. I guess you can do things like that when you live in a small town and have God on your side.

I had never been in the home of a priest before and I was absurdly relieved to see him standing at the top of the stairs wearing typical garb, black pants and black shirt with a white collar tab. If he had been wearing, say, a velour tracksuit I don't know whether I would have been able to say the things I needed to say.

Father Madrid was surprised to see me and I could tell that he remembered my face but absolutely nothing else about me, and definitely not my name.

"I'm Evangeline Lennon," I said. "Eva Lennon. Louise Lennon's granddaughter."

"Oh yes, of course. We all miss Louise. A terrible loss to the community."

I could tell that he didn't miss her at all. I supposed that he had presided over so many funerals that death no longer caused a feeling of unsurpassable loss inside him and I envied him that, the freedom to go on after a death and not have his life so completely rearranged.

"What can I do for you today?" he asked.

"If you don't mind, I'd like to talk to you for just a few minutes."

"I can't hear you, Evangeline, you'll have to come closer."

I was still in the middle of the stairway, a good five steps down from Father Madrid.

"I'm sorry, Father," I said, choosing my words with extra care. "I don't want you get overly excited, or inappropriately interested."

"What are you talking about?"

I'd given him fair warning, but as I brushed past him and walked into the apartment I heard him take a sharp inhale, and then I felt him walking just a little too close behind me.

"Can you do me a favor, Father, and put on your robe? It will make it a lot easier for me to talk with you."

In my mind the more layers he had on, the better.

Once he left the room I gave it a quick survey. I liked the Gothic look of his apartment. I believed that priests went very well with faded red velvet upholstery and decaying wood. His long drapes had a bit of black mold at the bottom where they touched the floor, his marble fireplace and blackened mantel mirror were dreary in a just-so manner, and his chandelier held real candles that looked as though they had actually been lit, and were not there purely for show.

Father Madrid returned wearing an ankle-length, white linen vestment, the kind he wore for Mass, and together with his thick salt-and-pepper hair, and long, silver cross hanging around his neck, he looked like the priest I remembered from church.

"Is this better?" he asked.

"Much," I said.

"Let's sit down and have a talk, then, shall we?"

He patted the cushion next to him on the worn-out sofa.

"Okay, well, I'll just dive right in because my boyfriend, Gabriel, like the angel," I said, tipping Father Madrid off to the fact that I had, at some point, gone to church and heard his sermon, "is waiting for me at home. We're leaving for New Orleans today."

"That's where your grandmother was from? Am I correct?"

"That's right."

"Go ahead, then."

I settled myself on the couch.

"When Louise died she left a gift for me inside her house. I didn't find it until after she passed and I thought since you knew her pretty well and for such a long time, you might know something about it."

"I just might. What did she leave for you?"

"This," I said, sitting down right next to him.

"I don't see anything, Evangeline. What is it that you're showing me?"

I moved closer. I sat so close to Father Madrid that the sides of our thighs were touching.

"I don't understand," he said, but I could feel his thigh pressing back against mine, just a little bit, which I accepted as a matter of course due to the scent and didn't hold against him in any way.

"Can you smell the scent of jasmine and red velvet rose?" I asked.

"Yes, yes I can," he said, "very much so. I remember now that it was Louise's favorite. The church pews at her funeral held this very same scent. It took us forever to get it out of the woodwork."

"And the fire and the leather, can you smell that too?"

Father Madrid closed his eyes.

"I think I can," he said.

"It was a perfume that she left me, Father. A very special scent that she made just for me."

"It's beautiful," he said. "Such an extraordinary gift."

"It's much more than that, Father. Its beauty is the least interesting thing about it."

"Tell me," he said in his most paternal voice, the one I recognized from the inside of the confessional.

"I'm certain it's a permanent part of my body now, maybe even a part of my soul. It never goes away, or washes off, or changes, or fades. Ever. It's exactly the same as when I first put it on and I believe at this point it may be coming from inside of me and seeping out, through my skin. This scent, this everlasting perfume, this is what she left for me when she died. She gave me something that lasts forever."

Father Madrid was silent for a moment.

"If there's one thing I've learned," he said, "it's that nothing lasts forever, not you, or I, certainly not your grandmother, or the scent on your skin. Only God, the Holy Spirit, continues on."

"One of the last things she told me was that perfume is not a thing, but the spirit of a thing," I said.

"Do you think she left you a spirit?" he asked. "Perhaps even her own?"

"I don't know. That's why I'm here."

Father Madrid put his fingertips together and looked up at the ceiling.

"This wasn't at all what I was expecting," he said.

"It wasn't what I was expecting either."

"When I heard the buzzer I thought it would be the usual drug problem or teenage pregnancy."

He sounded annoyed.

"What is it that you want from me?" he asked. "What do you want me to do about this gift from your grandmother?"

"I thought that maybe you could help me figure out what it is, its spiritual nature, its chemistry, and why it never leaves my body."

Father Madrid leaned in so close that the silver cross dangling from his neck touched my knees.

"If you must know, I believe it's a warning," he said.

I was alarmed.

"About what?"

Father Madrid stood up from the couch, his face flushed.

"How could I know such a thing?"

"You knew her for a long time."

"I'm sorry to say I don't have a clue. I'm just very glad you didn't come to St. Agnes to see me. You would have disrupted my sermon and disturbed the entire congregation with your . . . scent."

"I can't just stay away from other people, Father. And besides, even if I wanted to, they can't seem to get enough of being near me."

Father Madrid motioned with his hand as if he were brushing away the air in front of him.

"This is nothing more than the devil's game. A trick. A way to lure the wrong types of people toward you."

"Do you think Louise gave me something evil?"

"Maybe she gave you something to teach you a lesson. I honestly don't know, and as she has already passed it's too late for us to find out now, isn't it?"

Father Madrid walked toward the door and held it open and I looked up at him from the couch.

"Are you asking me to leave?"

"I can't help you, Evangeline Lennon. The only advice I can offer you is to try to stay in during the daylight hours and go out as late as possible at night, preferably when the rest of us are sleeping. At least until this scent, whatever it is, wears off."

I started the slow climb down the stairs. I'm not sure what it was that I expected from my visit, but this was not it.

"Evangeline," he called to me.

I stopped, but I didn't turn around. I knew that if I looked at Father Madrid I might believe what he said about Louise having an evil intent.

"Hop between the drops," he said. "Outrun the darkening sky. Stay out of the rain."

"What?"

"I have no idea," said Father Madrid. "I don't know what I just said."

࿊

I left the apartment and stepped out into an almost perfect circle of sunshine on the street. I understood, standing there in the light, that it was a mistake to see Father Madrid. Now that I was leaving Cyril he was part of my past. He knew I should stay out of the rain, but like me, he didn't know why, so he was of no use. He was as lost as I was and the last thing I needed in my life was a lost priest.

29

The New Orleans airport was strangely empty. It was raining when we walked outside through the revolving doors, pouring so hard that I was not bothered by the sound of the drops—there were simply too many of them, so many that they made one single pounding sound on the sidewalk instead of the individual drip, drip, drip that was like a noose around my brain.

And then, just as I was used to the sound, the rain stopped, suddenly, the way it does in summer in the south, and the drops were again dripping, one by one, off the treetops and onto the windshield and hood of the cab we were in, sending shivers through my mind.

"Don't worry," said Gabriel, "there aren't many trees in the French Quarter. When it rains, it won't always be like this."

He took my hand.

"You know what makes me feel this way?" I asked.

"I do. It's the ones you can hear individually. The single drops."

✌

The cab pulled up to our building on St. Louis between Decatur and Chartres Streets, a three-story cement stucco town house in the old creole style. It was painted pale pink and covered with delicate ironwork like a lace veil. It had an arched opening with a wrought-iron gate and an old metal lock.

Inside, the ground-floor hallway had high, rounded ceilings and a dark caramel tiled floor leading to a garden in the back. It was drippy and heavy with the scent of jasmine, just like me.

Wisteria rolled down from the top-floor balconies all the way to the garden below and curled around the legs of the iron tables and chairs like beautiful prison shackles. Everything about the building looked like it was from another century, and having never been to New Orleans I did not yet know that everything was.

I waited for Gabriel to get the bags out of the car and then we walked up the stairs to the second floor. Like a friendly greeting, the door to our apartment was open and an old-fashioned chandelier was visible from the stairs. It was the kind with real candles like the one in Father Madrid's apartment and it hung from the ceiling of the living room on a thick gold chain.

There were enormous arched Palladium windows flooding the living and dining rooms with light and heat, and floors of wide-planked dark wood.

"Tell me about your painter friend," I said, opening a door that led out onto a balcony overlooking the garden. I wanted to know what he was like, this man who owned such a beautiful apartment but chose not to live inside of it.

"You can see for yourself the day after tomorrow. We're going to meet him at the Broken Heart Ballroom. It's a country music hall. Kind of a legend in New Orleans."

Gabriel walked out onto the balcony and stood next to me.

"But if you really want to know, our first meeting was a bit strange and I found myself thinking about it at the most inconvenient times, like when I was at the library or in class."

"How so?"

"It was in a café in the Quarter when I first saw him. I was taking a study break and he noticed my white lab coat. He introduced himself without any hesitation. No fear of approaching a total stranger."

Gabriel stared out over the garden without turning to look at me as if he were remembering out loud instead of having an actual conversation.

"He wanted to know what the human body looked like . . . on the inside. He said that painters need to know as much about anatomy as doctors do, but they never get to see it up close."

"What did you tell him?"

"All kinds of things. I found myself confessing to him, telling him things I don't normally talk about with anyone. I told him about the thick, rubbery skin of the cadavers in the lab and the horrible smell of chemical preservative, which eventually goes away, and also about the guilt of cutting into another person, which never does."

I remembered Gabriel telling me that a certain number of medical students drop out after their first year because they know they can't spend their lives around the dead. Others discover they're allergic to formaldehyde and their careers are cut short that way. And then there are the ones who go into forensics so they can be around death all the time. "A special breed," he called them.

"Have you seen his paintings?" I asked.

"Some occult stuff," said Gabriel. "Voodoo priestesses, werewolves, pentagrams, things like that. But mostly he sits in the park and paints regular people. Portraits. He's pretty well known around here but he admitted to me right away that he never achieved the kind of fame he thought he would."

"Why do you think?"

"Hard to say. I liked his paintings well enough, but his faces were just faces, and his flowers just flowers. There was nothing truly original. At least nothing that I could see. It made me think of heart surgeons that I've studied. Some create entirely new valves that allow people to live years longer than they should, and others just put those valves in place, patient after patient. They're both surgeons, but they're not the same."

30

It was midnight of our first day in the Crescent City when Gabriel and I finally left the apartment on St. Louis. The one thing Father Madrid and I were in agreement about was that it would probably be best if I went out after dark when there were fewer people on the streets, and less chance of my scent being detected, at least for a little while.

Walking around the Quarter with its horses and buggies, cobblestone streets, and kerosene lamps felt like stepping back in time, all the way back to the time when Louise was a small child living in Fayetteville. I imagined her in a linen jumper with a white collar, skipping along the cobblestones, avoiding the cracks that would break her mother's back.

It was quiet outside as sweltering August temperatures kept tourists off the streets and residents inside their homes. The blocks felt private and sensual as Gabriel and I held hands and walked under the lush vegetation spilling from the baskets that hung off the balconies of the houses on St. Philip.

I could smell the sweet olive and the jasmine and I had the pleasant sensation of knowing that they were coming from outside of my body. New Orleans was my equal in scent, and as long as it was night and the air was a degree or two cooler than in the daytime I was sure I could walk around freely without attracting any unwanted attention.

We made a left on Burgundy and Gabriel stopped in the middle of the block and held my hand tight.

"Let's go in there," he said.

He pointed up at a parlor-floor apartment with a light coming through the window and a heavy wooden door that was partially open. The sign on the outer gate was written in a unique and beautiful longhand: *Come Inside Mes Amis. Madame Susteen Will Create a Scent Especially for You.*

I was surprised by Gabriel's desire, as the exotic world of a scent shop did not seem like a place he would naturally gravitate toward.

"I'm sure she could never create anything as beautiful as Louise did," I said.

"Of course not, Evangeline, that did not even cross my mind. But maybe she can smell your skin and tell us what was in the ruby vial."

There it was again, that thought, stealthy and constant, forever maneuvering its way back into my mind: What did Gabriel want?

What was he interested in? Was it me, or the science experiment that I had become? From the beginning he had had a curiosity, almost an obsession, about what was inside the vial, and I could still detect a certain intellectual restlessness around the topic.

"I didn't know you were still thinking about ingredients," I said.

"Don't you want to know too?"

The truth was that I did not. I wanted to live inside of this gift from Louise that had brought me Gabriel and now the beautiful city of New Orleans. I watched as my life changed day by day and I didn't want to dissect the scent and possibly render it understand-able and ordinary. I suppose that when it came to the ruby vial, magic meant more to me than science.

But still, from time to time I wondered about the part of the scent I could not name. It plagued my unconscious mind, sitting there like a sealed envelope. Father Madrid had called it a warning, and I had called it the scent of darkness. Maybe in the middle of the night this woman on Burgundy Street would know the unknown.

As I reached for the door Gabriel stopped and kissed me, which was really more like breathing me in, which had become his way of kissing.

"It's just for fun," he said to the back of my neck. "Madame Susteen, whoever she is, could never create anything as beautiful as this."

I laughed. I had been all filled up with Father Madrid and rain-drops and hidden warnings when in reality I was standing on a cobblestone street under a crescent moon with my dark-haired angel, Gabriel.

31

The woman behind the counter in Madame Susteen's scent parlor clicked her long nails on the glass countertop.

"I thought you were going to kiss in front of my store forevah," she said in a distinctly southern accent, dropping the r at the end of the word forever, "and that's a long time to be looking at the two of you. I can tell you that right now."

"No ma'am," said Gabriel. "We weren't going to kiss for that long. It was just our way of deciding whether or not to come inside."

Gabriel spoke to the woman with a sudden southern accent of his own. She stared at him, hardly noticing me, and seemed to take to him on sight. I thought it was a good sign and so I kept quiet about the new sound of his voice.

"Well, you two look around all you like," she said. "Take your time. I'm here all night long, evah night of the week. If you don't find what you're looking for tonight, there's always tomorrah night, and the one after that."

She winked at Gabriel.

"What do they call you, back east?" she asked.

"I'm Gabriel, and this is Evangeline."

"Gabriel and Evangeline. Verah religious names you both have. Why is that?"

"I don't know," I said. "I've never thought about it that way."

"Well, start thinking about it. Nothing's for nothing."

"Are you Madame Susteen, like the sign?"

"The one and only."

Aside from the long glass countertop the shop looked like someone's living room, with two worn blue velvet couches and dark velvet curtains pulled aside to reveal smaller rooms beyond, with scuffed wooden floors and dormer windows.

Besides the usual crosses nailed to the walls and pictures of the voodoo queen Marie Laveau that I'd seen in every book about New Orleans, Madame Susteen's store had rows and rows of dusty bottles filled with different oily-looking liquids, which I imagined to be her scented creations. These were not the kind of perfectly designed perfume bottles you would find in department stores but ones that looked as if they had been carefully collected over years and years, with big, rounded bellies and cut-glass stoppers, and jars so unique they could have filled a store in their own right even if they had held nothing but air.

"What's in them?" I asked.

"Nothing you'd be interested in."

"How do you know?"

"Because I know."

"So, we've got something to ask you," said Gabriel, putting his fingertips together in a prayer position, with what I imagined was a position of deference to the rather overpowering presence of Madame Susteen.

"Don't be shy," she said, turning her back to us and fixing her hair in a round mirror on a silver stand behind her chair. "Talk to me, boy."

She wrapped and pinned her long braids into the highest pile of hair I'd seen on anyone since Louise, but I got the feeling she was not interested in fixing them at all, but that she was simply taking the opportunity to look at us more closely in the rear view of the mirror.

"The higher the hair, the closer to God," she said. "Did you know that?"

"I did," I said. "My grandmother used to say that. She had the highest hair I'd ever seen until right now."

"You'd be lucky to be half as smart as your grandmother," she said, spinning around in her chair, facing us, "but I'm sure that you are not. Now, what can I do for two young folks such as yourselves out in the Quartah so late?"

Madame Susteen was a stranger in a strange shop. But with her high hair and southern accent she was closer to Louise than anyone I'd ever met. I felt comfortable with her and also uncomfortable, just the way I had with Louise.

"I was given a scent as a gift from my grandmother, who was from these parts, a place called Fayetteville, and I thought maybe you could tell me, us, what it's made of."

"Fayetteville, huh? I've got a story to tell you all about a woman from Fayetteville," said Madame Susteen. "She was the best aromata who ever lived. They say she was a Creole from West Africa with Indian blood in her too. And when she walked down the street from parish to parish the women would line up along the road waiting for just one sweet drop of her sweat to fall. They'd take that teeny bit of liquid and scrub it into their skin until they were raw and bleeding. She smelled so good they were trying to get it directly into their own bloodstream."

"I think my grandmother knew that woman," I said. "She told me about someone like that once. She said every living creature would come out to see her. Even the ants would dance around their anthills when they caught a whiff of her scent on the breeze."

"So where is this perfume from your grandmother?"

I stuck out my arm.

"I think it's inside of my skin."

Madame Susteen looked at my outstretched arm.

"She didn't tell you what was in the perfume?"

"She didn't have time. I found it after she died."

"That's a pity, sweetheart. I'm sorry to tell you that I don't breathe in anyone's scent directly from the body. I learned a long time ago that it's altogether too possible to get trapped with a person, stuck with them forevah, just by inhaling their scent. I don't do it anymore. No ma'am. I'm too old and experienced for all of that. I can make one for you, though, any scent you like. I'll mix you something that'll keep this beautiful boy right here by your side for the rest of your life. Or maybe something that'll bring you more money than you evah dreamed. Babies too. I can do all of that. But don't stick your skinny arm out in front of me. A scent isn't a thing, it's the spirit of a thing, and I don't need no stranger's spirit living inside of me."

Madame Susteen put her hands on her hips and looked us both up and down.

"At least not until I know exactly who you are," she added, as if on second thought.

"That could take a long time," I said.

"There are other ways besides talking," she said, patting a few stray hairs into place, "but it'll cost you."

"I have some money," said Gabriel.

Madame Susteen smiled and her large white teeth made the inside of her mouth look like a lightbulb.

"No matter how much you have, boy, it's going to cost you more than that."

She reached down underneath the cash register and came up with a deck of cards.

"You evah had your fortune told?"

Gabriel shook his head no while I pondered the uncanny cross between Louise and Rosemary that Madame Susteen had suddenly become.

"The tarot will tell me all I need to know. It's quicker than talking to you and a lot more accurate too. It can take a lifetime to tease and pick the truth out of the things people tell you about themselves. Believe me, honey, people lie all the time. I know. Now, why don't you go ahead and shuffle the deck. If we're extra lucky the cards might even tell us something about that scent your grandmother left you."

I looked at Gabriel.

"Why don't you go first," I said. "There must be some things you want to know too?"

"That's right, boy," said Madame Susteen. "You look like a nice sort. I'm sure the cards won't have a bad word to say about you."

Gabriel took the deck.

"I just want to tell you, Madame Susteen, I'm a medical student. No offense, but I don't believe in this stuff at all. Not one word of it."

"I know you don't, son, but try anyway, just for the fun of it. Go ahead and live a little."

Gabriel shuffled only once and handed the deck back to Madame Susteen.

"Hmmm. It takes a confident young man to shuffle just one time. I think I'll do a Raven's Eye for you. It's the type of spread that shows where you are, where you should be, where you will be at some point in the future, and, of course, what to avoid."

She spread six cards facedown, four on top and two below, and then began turning the top cards over one by one.

"Do you have any particular question for me?"

"I don't think so."

"You must have one. Evah man has at least one question buried deep inside of him. Dig down and I guarantee you'll find one in there somewhere."

Gabriel took his time thinking. I'll admit that I hoped that he would ask a question about me, about us, and our future.

"Okay," he said. "I'm studying medicine and pretty soon I'll have to pick a specialty. I'm interested in hematology and geriatrics. What kind of doctor should I be?"

Madame Susteen turned over three more cards and clicked her nails over and over on the glass countertop.

"Well, young man, this is rathah interesting and just when I thought I was going to be bored to tears. From where I sit it looks like you're going be a verah special kind of doctor."

"A surgeon?"

"Not exactly."

"An oncologist?"

"Nope, not that kind either."

"Tell me. What am I going to be?"

"Well, since you asked I'm going to give it to you straight. You may not like what I have to say but here it is. You're going to be a doctor of the dead."

"A what?"

"Don't look so alarmed, now. You're going to be a doctor who presides over the dead, that's all. The dead need doctors too. Just like evahbody else."

"I'm not going to be doctor of the dead. There's no such thing.

I'm going to help people avoid death for as long as they possibly can. That's my job."

Madame Susteen laughed with both hands on her thighs and her head facing down and shaking from side to side. When she looked up there were tears in her eyes.

"Avoid death? Now, that's a good one. You're a funny kid when you wanna be, you know that? Anyway, it's what the cards say, son, and I don't like when my clients blame me for the cards. Now, let me tell you a little story about a doctor I know. Maybe it'll make you feel better about your upcoming specialty."

"It's not my specialty."

Madame Susteen continued on in spite of Gabriel's agitation.

"I knew a man once who was aging and he hated it so. He was a verah wealthy man and he decided to do something about what he called his *affliction,* which was really just the natural passing of the years. He looked around long and hard until he found himself a doctor who would implement his plan. For a great sum of money he had all of his organs transplanted—replaced with those of a young car-crash victim who had just bled to death that same afternoon. The freshest, youngest organs he could find. In fact, we who know the man often wonder about that car crash. No one ever did find a cause."

"You mean the young man was murdered."

"For the verah organs in his body."

"How long did the older man live?"

"Oh, he's still living and breathing as sure as we're sitting here. He's old now, older than most folks evah get to be, but he's also verah young. His idea worked. He even had the pineal gland, located dead in the center of the brain, transplanted into his own head. In his mind there was no use having all those nice young organs without nice young hormones to go with them."

"I'm not buying a word of that story."

"I'm not selling it. I gave it to you for free. Just remember how it's done when you become a doctor of the dead. You could become famous, written up in all those textbooks, studied by all them fresh, young medical students coming up after you."

"The doctor in your story, why isn't he famous now?"

"Because the man paid him to be quiet. He wanted people to believe that he stayed so young because he was special, like some kind of rare breed of human being. It was a pact between the two of them. Part of the deal."

Madame Susteen smiled sweetly, almost perversely, considering what she'd just told Gabriel, and handed me the deck.

"Your turn, honey."

"These look hand-painted," I said, turning the cards over in my hands.

"These particular cards are old and rare. Handle them with care and they'll do the same for you."

"They didn't do that for me," said Gabriel.

"Shush, boy. Your time is over. Your question has been asked and answered. Let the cards move on away from you now. Don't suck off the rest of their energy before your girlfriend has a chance to hear what they have to say about her."

I shuffled the cards. They looked frayed and delicate, like paper gone through a wash cycle.

"This here is one of the oldest tarot decks in existence. It comes from a time way before TV and computers, even telephones, a time when people were more clairvoyant than they are today, when folks relied more on their natural-born instincts. These cards have kept me from mixing in with the wrong sort. I trust them like I trust my own child."

I started to put them down on the counter in front of Madame Susteen but she scooped them from my hands a second before they hit the glass.

"They have to come directly from you to me," she said. "Trust me. It works better that way."

She asked me to cut them with my left hand. I handed them to her and she spread the cards on the table, facedown.

"Pick nine cards and don't look at them."

I handed them back to her and she laid them out on the glass counter in the shape of a cross.

"Now turn them over, real careful. Remember, they're old and fragile just like you're going to be someday."

I slid my hand over each one as I turned it faceup.

I watched Madam Susteen's chest rise and fall with each breath. She didn't show her white teeth like she did when she looked at Gabriel's cards. Instead she pursed her lips and tapped her fingertips together.

"Verah strange. Verah strange indeed," she said. "Evah card you pulled is from the major arcana—the cards of the greater secrets and the deeper mysteries. When is your birthday, honey, if you don't mind my asking?"

"November 7, 1991."

"Hmmm . . . I like you, girl, so I hate to bring you bad news, but the cards don't lie and I won't lie for them, not for you, not even for people I like a whole lot more than you. Are you ready to know what they have to say?"

I didn't want to hear any bad news on my first night in New Orleans, but Madame Susteen placed her hands over mine, looked me in the eye, and went right on talking before I could answer.

"You were born in the first decan of Scorpio. A fated decan. A poor placement. Trouble, toil, and perhaps even death itself are in your cards. You're the child of the devil, a temptress and a seductress meant to lose love and hurt the ones who love you. You will bring much pain and possibly even death to others, or even to yourself if you're not careful."

Gabriel and I stood still in silent and total disbelief.

"Now I must ask you to leave," she said, with a firmness in her voice that could not be mistaken for anything but dislike. "Get out of my shop and never come back here again."

We backed away, not taking our eyes off Madame Susteen.

"Evangeline," she called out just before we crossed the threshold of the door, "I smelled you the second your foot touched down in New Orleans. I know what's in your grandmother's perfume. But if I tell you, you'll never understand for yourself the message she's trying to send. Find out what's in that scent. It's the key to changing the terrible, terrible nature of your cards."

"They can change?"

"Evahthing changes, honey. And Gabriel?"

"Yes," he said in a whisper.

"I never did get around to telling you what to avoid. One of your cards was the three of cups, normally a fine pick, but in your case it was reversed, upside down, a bad omen. You'll have to share your love, son, and it won't be your choice, or to your liking, to do so."

Outside the shop Gabriel and I tried to laugh off the reading. We strolled over to Bourbon Street hand in hand and bought hurricanes, the grain alcohol of choice for every tourist in the Quarter. We walked around drinking and laughing about our first night, making fun of Madame Susteen and her high hair and proper southern way of speaking. But the fortune stayed with us that night and all of the next day. It hung over us like a thunderstorm approaching. And no matter what we did we could not shake it off.

☙

"Back in Cyril you asked me to find a word for your scent," said Gabriel later that night in bed, "a word for how it made me feel when I was with you. I couldn't come up with one then—it was on the tip of my tongue but I couldn't find it."

"And now?" I asked.

"Heartbreaking. That's the word I was looking for. That's how it felt the first time we were together."

He was quiet for a moment.

"I hope it's not my heart that's going to break, Evangeline."

That night, for the first time, Gabriel and I did not touch. He buried his face in my hair like always but he did not come near my body and I was sure that I felt a chill run through me in the middle of the hot New Orleans summer night.

When I woke up the next morning Gabriel's side of the bed was cool and flat, as if he had left hours ago, before dawn. There was a note on his pillow about studying late at the Tulane Library and then meeting Michael Bon Chance.

It was somewhere around ninety-five degrees when I got out of bed so I slipped on the lightest thing I owned, a white cotton nightgown, and went downstairs. I opened the balcony door to a bright, sunny day. I leaned over the wrought-iron railing, drinking coffee and watching two kittens standing on their hind legs, playing with the wisteria hanging in the garden, while I eased into being awake, which was difficult in the thick, dreamy August air.

32

I walked past the Lost Love Lounge and the Dead Redhead before I found the Broken Heart Ballroom on the corner of Esplanade and Decatur. With a name that included the words "ballroom" and "broken heart" I had assumed the place would be cavernous and filled with hungry souls in search of each other for a lifetime, or even just a nighttime of company, but instead it was so small you could take in every single person from the doorway, feature for feature. There simply couldn't be that few broken hearts in the French Quarter of New Orleans.

The ballroom was a single square space. The floors were beaten up and covered with sawdust; signed pictures of country singers hung on the walls. From the doorway I could make out the signatures of Hank Williams, Patsy Cline, Willie Nelson, and Dolly Parton. They were larger-than-life people with large, exaggerated handwriting, and I spent a few minutes wondering if that were always the case.

My mind drifted back to the bar. I listened to Leonard Cohen's voice coming out of the jukebox singing a sad and lamenting ode to love lost and life passing by. As his voice rippled through the room like black silk, a mood hung over the bar, a sadness that drove people to drink whiskey, or red wine, and smoke too many cigarettes. It was clear that the Broken Heart was the kind of place that catered more to the memories of people than to the people themselves. Memories of wrong turns, opportunities missed, and big loves gone by. Standing in the doorway looking over the room I had to wonder if anyone ever ended up with the person they were supposed to.

My eyes landed on Gabriel. He was sitting on a stool with his back toward me and I saw him as if he were already gone. I looked at him that way for a while, trying to feel what I might feel if I'd lost him and then ran into him, perhaps here, in this very bar, years from now.

I tried not to treat us that way, I tried to pretend that I felt the way most people do when they're in love, as if it's going to last forever, but deep inside I didn't feel I could keep Gabriel for anything even close to forever. My mind always leaped to the future, a time when he would certainly be somewhere new with somebody else.

I closed the door behind me. Walking into the Broken Heart was like stepping into a melancholy feeling, and I had to wonder if this new person in our lives, Michael Bon Chance, had chosen it for that very reason.

I pulled my hair back into a ponytail with the black band I always kept on my wrist and shook off my pessimism. Louise had told me a long time ago that if you act in a certain way for long enough, eventually you'll be that way for real, so I put my arms around Gabriel from behind and acted as if he were really mine.

He swung around on his barstool and I stood between his legs as he brushed a few hairs that had escaped from the ponytail holder behind my ears.

A gust of hot air swept through the Broken Heart and I turned away from my love. A tall, handsome man with dark, wavy hair held the door open. He stood just over the threshold surveying the room, standing perfectly still in an attitude of command while the rest of us swayed to the music or finished off another round.

Heat flooded in from the outside, sucking the air-conditioning from the ballroom, replacing it with warm currents and making my scent rise up around me. Gabriel held me close. He remembered the party in Cyril and he protected me as best he could from the effects of my body on other people's minds. With his free hand he waved the man toward us. I closed my eyes and listened to the jukebox.

"This is Michael," said Gabriel, moving me away from his body.

I didn't want to but I opened my eyes and removed myself from the feel of Gabriel's chest.

Michael Bon Chance went to shake my hand but he changed his mind midway and bent all the way down and gave me a kiss on the cheek with full lips and large, dark eyes that stayed open no matter how close he came to my face.

The room was still warm, and with my scent on the rise I feared that he would linger, unable to pull away, and I did not want our first meeting to include his lips on my face. But I had nothing to worry about. He didn't comment on my scent or seem to notice it at all.

"Would you like to dance, Evangeline?" he asked with a little smile. Boyish and warm for a man so large and imposing.

I felt my face turn red and I was glad the bar was dark.

"I don't think so," I said.

"Why not? Are you shy?"

"No. I just met you, that's all."

"Come on then, let's all three of us dance," said Michael. He was upbeat and his happiness cut through the heavy mood of the Broken Heart like a balloon. "Let's get to know each other, landlord and tenants, shall we?"

"And friends," said Gabriel, "don't forget about friends."

"Of course," said Michael. "Friends."

Gabriel smiled at me, and shrugged his shoulders as if to say, There's nothing much we can do, it's his apartment we're living in, and then in one swift moment the three of us were standing next to the bar, dancing.

I was facing Gabriel and at the same time I could feel the breath of a man I'd just met on the back of my neck. As Nina Simone sang "Wild Is the Wind" he slipped his honey-colored hands around my waist. Gabriel put his lips on my cheek and against my wishes the feeling of being in between the two of them moved ever so slowly from bad to good.

When Dolly Parton started singing "Jolene," a song about love being stolen away, Gabriel steered us back to our seats. I could see the bartender and more than a few other people glancing over at the three of us and thinking things that weren't true.

"You're a good dancer, Evangeline. A beautiful dancer," said Michael.

"Slow down, buddy," said Gabriel.

"I'm just saying she has something special. She's a beautiful girl, yes, anybody can see that, but she also possesses *beauté de l'âme,* a beauty of the soul."

"That's quite a sentence," Gabriel said, looking at me as if *I'd* said something wrong.

"She has the powers of a sorceress," continued Michael, talking to Gabriel as if I were not in the room but knowing perfectly well that I was listening to every word he said. "I felt it when we were dancing, and I've lived in New Orleans long enough to know."

"She's from New York," said Gabriel, "upstate New York. Take my word for it, there aren't a lot of sorceresses up there."

I felt like saying that wasn't true, that Louise was one, but I said nothing.

"New Orleans can change a person," said Michael, "like from someone ordinary into someone extraordinary."

"Not in two nights," said Gabriel.

"It's been known to happen. I've seen it with my own eyes. Anyway, I didn't mean to offend. It was a simple compliment to your girlfriend. A New Orleans greeting, if you will."

"Well, give it to your own girlfriend, then, not mine."

Michael took two steps back and put his hands up in front of him.

"No worries, my friend and tenant. You'll never hear me say it again."

Just then, the woman standing on my left, a redhead in a pink dress with silver sparkles on her eyelids, tapped me on the shoulder.

"What are you're wearing?" she asked. "What's the name of your perfume?"

"I don't remember," I said. "I bought it a long time ago."

Gabriel smiled.

"Can I smell it?"

I nodded and she leaned toward my neck and put her nose against my jugular vein just as Rayanne had under the weeping willow tree in Cyril.

"That's real good," she said in a deep, quiet voice, leaning toward me again, coming in for a second time around. "Do you mind?"

"No," I said, pulling my ponytail to the other side of my neck. I already knew the tip of her tongue was going reach out to touch the mark of the vial on my skin and I didn't want its wetness on my hair. The girl leaned in again and just as I thought her tongue came out straight away and caressed my skin. I could feel it flicking back and forth across my vein.

"What are you doing?" asked her friend on the next barstool.

She pulled herself away from my skin.

"Come here, you have to smell this."

The next thing I knew I had two girls, a redhead and a blonde, one on either side of me, with their soft lips against my neck. Michael stared at me, fascinated, while Gabriel was looking out at the dance floor as if he couldn't wait for the night to be over.

"May I have a turn?" asked Michael.

"You can smell *my* perfume," said the girl with the pink dress, hoping the sparkles on her eyelids would hold a power over Michael that she knew her own irises could not.

"Maybe next time," he said to her while looking at me.

"Go ahead," I said, resigned. I knew the time would come sooner or later and I wanted to get it over with right there, preferably in a room filled with people.

I looked at Gabriel. He rolled his eyes, then nodded.

Michael moved in slow motion, as though he was getting ready to savor something special. He moved in, in that unnerving way he had, without closing his eyes, and then he put his nose against my neck in the same spot they all did.

He pulled back much sooner than I thought he would, almost immediately, and he looked surprised.

"I don't smell anything," he said.

I looked at Gabriel and I could see the relief in his eyes.

Michael turned to the girl with the sparkles.

"Your turn now."

He held her hair away from her neck and put his nose against her throat.

"You smell like innocence."

"That's not a scent," she said.

I knew Louise would beg to differ.

The girl smiled at him, thinking she might have a successful night at the Broken Heart after all.

"Don't look so happy," said Michael. "My taste runs more toward the exotic."

"Cruel," whispered Gabriel, but my mind had stopped five minutes earlier and all I could think about was that he could not detect Louise's scent on my body. I felt conflicted. Both disappointed, as if I'd failed at something that was a God-given talent, and at the same time, free of that very same gift. Unencumbered and more like my old self than I'd felt in a long time. As if I was just a woman, and Michael was just a man in a bar who had been attracted to me because I could dance. Simple. The way it's supposed to be.

"We're leaving now," said Gabriel, signaling for the check, "while we still have the chance," he said, more to himself than to me.

He left to pay the bill while I stood in place still feeling the rejection and the freedom of Michael's inability to notice me. I finally headed for the door, but Michael put his hand on my waist.

"Where are you going?"

"Home."

"Why the rush? We're just getting to know each other. Landlord and tenant," he said, smiling. "And friend."

"What do you want to know?"

Michael laughed uncomfortably.

"You're very direct."

"I am," I said, even though in truth I so rarely was.

"Well, to start with, I'm a portrait painter."

"I've heard."

"To be honest, I was thinking, or hoping, that maybe you would sit for me sometime. I'm sure you don't know many people in New Orleans, and with Gabriel in school I thought you might like some company."

His hand on my arm gave me a chill, which finally brought my scent down to a manageable level. I looked over at Gabriel, who had paid the bill and was staring at the door as if he were willing a huge gust of wind to sweep the two of us out of the Broken Heart.

"Next time the drinks are on me," Michael said to Gabriel.

"Damn right they are," Gabriel said under his breath.

Michael bent down and gave me a quick kiss on the cheek.

"Think about it," he said. "At the very least you'll end up with a painting, and maybe even a new friend."

ॐ

Gabriel and I left the Broken Heart and walked until we found Burgundy Street, where I stopped and looked up at the window of Madame Susteen's parlor-floor scent shop.

"Don't do that," he said. "It will bring us bad luck."

We walked in silence until he was able to ask the question that I could tell had been on his mind all night: "So what do you think?" he asked. "Of Michael?"

The truth would be too vague and perhaps too positive to please Gabriel, so I went with a portion of the truth that would satisfy him, although I was not altogether sure if truth had portions.

"If you and I were not together I wouldn't choose him as a boyfriend, if that's what you're asking."

"Maybe not at first," said Gabriel, "but he gets to people, you know? They line up in the park, in the cold, in the rain, just so he can paint them. Especially women. I've seen it myself."

"You don't have anything to worry about," I said. "He doesn't even notice my scent."

"You sound disappointed."

"I'm not."

"What do you want to do now?" asked Gabriel,

"It's three in the morning," I said. "I want to go home."

"That's too bad, because I've been waiting my turn all night long."

Gabriel pulled me onto his lap on the steps of the courthouse on St. Louis. He flicked his tongue across the veins of my neck the way the girls in the Broken Heart had.

"Tell me," he asked, "did it feel good when they did it?"

"It did."

He bit harder into my neck.

"I could tell," he said.

As night rolled into morning, I knew it in my bones. Our trip to New Orleans was fated. Very soon it would be impossible to go back to being who we were before. I held on tight to Gabriel until the sun came up. I couldn't help thinking I was going to be sipping bourbon, smoking cigarettes, and dreaming of him at the bar in the Broken Heart Ballroom, long after he was gone.

33

The bed was messy the next morning, the sheets tangled up with the blankets in a long snaking coil of white cotton, and the carpeting damp from a bottle of water that had been knocked off the nightstand. The spell that Madame Susteen had put on Gabriel and me, the negativity and the weirdness of it that had continued right on into the Broken Heart Ballroom, had finally been broken during the long, sensual, early morning hours.

Gabriel had already left for school and I was standing over the balcony drinking the chicory-flavored coffee that was everywhere in New Orleans, when there was a knock at the door.

It was so hot I didn't even bother to cover myself up and when I opened the door I was sorry because there was a young boy standing in the hallway. He was maybe thirteen or fourteen years old, tall and thinly elegant as only very young teenagers can be.

I looked him up and down. He had a perfect blend of unidentifiable ethnicities that together hinted at great future beauty: golden bronze skin, large black eyes, and dark blond hair that trailed all the way down his back to his waist. The length and wildness of his hair made him look motherless.

He leaned against the wall with one hand as if he were holding it up, and in the other he had a white cupcake covered with multicolored sprinkles.

"We live across the hall," he said. "My mama says to say hello." He held the cupcake toward me. "This is for you."

"That's very nice of her," I said pulling my nightgown down around my thighs. "Why didn't she bring it over herself?"

"She said that's what kids are for. To run errands for their parents."

"She sounds just like my mother."

"You look too old to have a mama."

"Thanks."

I took the cupcake from his hand and we stood in the doorway looking at each other without saying anything, me in my white nightdress and him in his white undershirt and low-slung pants with maroon boxers sticking out of the waistband, like two neighbors who'd known each other forever, or a woman and her very illegal lover saying goodbye to each other for the coming day.

"Can I come in for a while?" he asked. "We don't have air-conditioning at our place."

"Maybe another time," I said.

"Like when?"

"I don't know. Whenever you feel like it."

I knew as soon as the words were out of my mouth that they were a mistake.

"You smell kinda good, lady. Even better than the baby next door, and everybody says she smells real good."

"Thanks."

"See ya."

"Yes. See you later."

With the door closed I bit into the cupcake. The frosting was waxy and coated the roof of my mouth with chemicals and sugar. I was putting paste on my toothbrush, getting ready to scrape it off, when there was another knock on the door.

"Who is it?" I yelled from the bathroom.

"It's me again. From across the hall."

I opened the door.

"My mama says you need to go to the cemetery today."

"What?"

"She says that all tourists go there and that you should go to St. Serafina in the Bywater and bring this with you."

He dug a small object out of the front pocket of his jeans and held it in his palm for me to see. I bent over for a closer look. It was a ceramic finger, an index finger, bent at the joint, with a long red nail attached to the end.

"It's a thank-you for the saint who fixed the arthritis in my mama's hand. The nail on the end is her own. She grew it real long then pulled it off and glued it on here, just like they do at the nail shops. She says to leave it in the chapel on your way out."

I took the finger from his hand and without turning around I placed it behind me in a silver bowl on the table by the door where we kept a set of spare keys. It sat there like a hideous new key ring.

"Where is your mother now?"

"In bed."

"Tell her I'll do my best to get the finger to the chapel, but it's really hot outside and I may not make it over there today."

"Didn't you read the sign on the church across the street?" he asked.

"Not yet."

"It says: *Sure it's hot outside today, but hell is hotter.*"

But it's not this humid, I thought to myself.

"Are you scared of the cemetery?" he asked.

"Not really."

"Dead people can't hurt you, you know. It's the ones that are alive that you gotta watch out for."

"That's a good point," I said. "What's your name, anyway?"

"Levon. What's yours?"

"Evangeline."

"Evangeline. That's a nice name. Well, see ya later."

"Hey, Levon, let's see each other another day. Not today, okay?"

"Sure. I'll come back tomorrow and see how you liked the cemetery. I go there to think sometimes. It's cool and quiet. You'll like it there. I know you will."

I watched him slip into his apartment and then I got back to doing the only two things I'd done since I'd arrived in New Orleans— drinking coffee and looking out over the balcony at the garden below. The heat made me sleepy and I went inside to take a long afternoon nap.

34

It was hours later when I finally woke and the apartment walls were colored in pink and red from the late afternoon sun. I wondered if Levon had put some kind of spell on me, or if his mother had put something stronger than sugar into the cupcake gift.

I dressed fast. I wanted to make it to the cemetery before it closed. I didn't want to have to sneak in but I also wanted to make sure I got rid of the finger before the day was over.

St. Serafina was an old, dilapidated cemetery surrounded by a high, rusted iron gate. It was crisscrossed with twisted dirt paths that came to sudden, silent dead ends at crumbling tombs. The crosses and statues that sat high on the tombs shed eerie shadows that looked like sinkholes in the ground, but to me it was not at all scary. I had spent so much time over the years eating lunch against the gravestones in Cyril that cemeteries did not have the same kind of meaning for me as they did for other people. I found them comforting instead of frightening. They reminded me of Louise and the Stone Crow.

There were differences, though. New Orleans is below sea level so the graves can't be put into the ground. I read somewhere that they used to try to put the coffins in the dirt but as soon as it rained they would rise up to the surface and get stuck in the mud or simply float away. People would walk out of their houses to find a coffin or, even worse, a corpse, sitting out on their front lawn right next to the wisteria tree, first thing in the morning.

I took a walk through the rows of tombs and vaults that looked like blocks and blocks of dead people living next door to each other in the quietest neighborhood that ever existed. There were mausoleums as big as some of the houses I'd seen in the Garden District. Some were well taken care of, whitewashed, and covered with small offerings. Others had huge marble statues of angels holding flowers. And a few were moldy and decayed with actual bones sticking up through the cracks. That was something I had *never* seen in Cyril.

On the opposite side of the cemetery, far from the entrance, a large Christ on the cross was guarding the door to the chapel where I was supposed to put the finger. I hoped it was open so I wouldn't have to carry it around with me all night long. I passed Jesus and pushed on the door. There was no light inside, but hundreds of tiny candles threw off enough of a glow for me to get the job done.

In the dim light of the votives I could see that the walls were covered with offerings far more gruesome than the one I had in my pocket. There were rows of plaster feet hanging on the walls representing all sorts of problems: missing toes and mangled ankles, black toenails, fungus, and gangrene. There was a small ear stuffed into a test tube, a thin lock of gray hair tied with twine, glass eyeballs, and tumorous-looking things in jars, perhaps stillborn babies or body parts that I didn't want to get too close to. I found an empty space on a table next to two doll heads glued together with the names Ellis and John written on their foreheads in marker pen, and laid the finger down. The red nail polish had chipped on the way over and I hoped that wouldn't affect the outcome for Levon's mother. I lit a candle for the continued success of her arthritis treatment, and left.

By the time I got outside it was dark. I called Gabriel.

"Where are you?" he asked.

"In a cemetery in the Bywater."

"Feeling homesick?"

I smiled a secret smile that I knew he could see over the phone.

"Do you want to meet for dinner?" I asked.

"Yeah. Let's go somewhere nice. I've been in the library for eight hours studying birth defects. I need you, and a lot of alcohol."

"Follet on St. Louis?"

"Perfect. And please take a cab. I know you like to walk, but do me the favor."

"Of course," I said and then immediately started walking.

I was enjoying a slow crawl through the dark, quiet streets of the Marigny, past parks half beautiful and half broken, like microcosms of New Orleans itself, quiet churches, used bookstores, and cafés.

I turned onto Chartres Street, one of my favorites so far, and stopped to peek through the pale green shutters of an abandoned boardinghouse. I could make out iron cots, school desks with inkwells, and old leather trunks that must have held clothing and blankets. I wanted to stay and imagine who could have lived inside, but the sound of footsteps on the empty street caught my attention. They were slow but purposeful, and loud against the dead quiet of the neighborhood.

I held my bag tight against my body and walked away as quickly as I could, but it didn't matter how fast I went because the footsteps continued to come closer until I knew for sure that I was in danger. I knew it because I could feel it in my heartbeat. I quickened my pace but there was something strange about the speed of the person behind me. It was the footsteps. They never changed. They had the same slow cadence they had when I first heard them. No matter how fast I went they managed to stay near me, close behind, making me feel as if I weren't moving at all.

When my fear level became unmanageable I broke into a run, and just as I got to the corner I felt something ice cold on my arm, like a bony hand peeking out from a grave in the cemetery. I tried to talk but nothing came out of my mouth. I turned around and looked into the face of Michael Bon Chance.

He put his arm around my shoulders, which I was relieved to see was a normal, human arm after all, and pulled us back against the wooden door of a closed bookstore. I was breathing fast and my heart was pounding so hard that it wouldn't have surprised me if it broke through my chest and fell onto the street in front of me.

"Evangeline, relax," he said. "Take a deep breath. I called out to you but you didn't hear me. You were in your own little world."

"What are you doing here?" I asked, hoping the panic I felt didn't leak into my voice.

"Gabriel called me and told me you were at the cemetery. He wanted to know if you would be able to get a cab at this time in this neighborhood. I knew you wouldn't, so I came as fast as I could."

I stared at him, hardly believing a word he said. He didn't seem winded and I was still fighting for every morsel of air I could find.

"Let's keep walking," I said.

"Slow down and catch your breath. I think we should stand still for a moment. Would that be okay?"

I released the white-knuckle grip I had on my bag.

"I was visiting the cemetery," I said. "I guess it got to me more than I thought it would."

"No worries. I understand," he said.

"Thanks for coming to meet me."

"Not a problem."

We walked down the street in silence and at the corner I changed the subject and asked him if he'd found someone to sit for him.

"I haven't," he said. "Have you given it any more thought?"

"Not really," I admitted. "Not since the Broken Heart."

"Just a few hours is all I need, and it'll be a lot more fun than a day at the cemetery. Plus, you owe me now that I've rescued you from the dangers of Chartres Street."

I laughed, looking out at the quiet street around me.

"I guess I do. But from what Gabriel tells me, a lot of women want to sit for you. So why me?"

Michael stopped walking.

"A lot of reasons," he said, "But mostly I want to capture a full body this time, not just the face, like I do in the park."

"I don't want to be captured by you."

He stood away from me and took both of my hands in his.

"It's just a figure of speech, Evangeline. All painters use it. It's hard to get a woman to come to the studio because I'm not a famous artist. I'm a stranger and a man and they get nervous about being alone with me. Anyway, aren't you bored at home all day?"

He had me there. I was bored. And lonely too. In fact, I was so bored that I'd actually gone to a cemetery to deliver a finger and so lonely that I was looking forward to the company of a fourteen-year-old boy more than I cared to admit. Loneliness like that could be dangerous.

"I'm sure that I could create something very beautiful from your image. Something we could both love," he said.

In a turnaround of feeling I found myself liking Michael Bon Chance just a little bit more than I had thought possible. I could tell that he was attracted to something inside of me, some innate quality that I possessed. He needed something from me that was mine alone and did not come out of a red teardrop in a white room. There was a certain level of freedom I felt talking to him there on Chartres Street in the dark. It was the way I used to feel before the white room and the vial and the note.

I could already picture the days to come. I would no longer spend them walking around the Quarter alone, waiting for Gabriel to come home from school. Instead I would become a muse for a portrait painter. The more I thought about it the more I liked that particular description of myself.

"Will you have dinner with Gabriel and me?"

"I'd love to, but no," he said. "Can I expect to see you tomorrow? We can talk more about the painting. We can collaborate on it if you'd like. I'm open to any ideas you might have."

"Tomorrow, then," I said.

As he walked away I realized that I'd been holding his cold palms in mine for too many long, inappropriate moments.

Maybe it was the temperature of his hands that stopped him from being a great painter. Too cool and distant. Not enough blood and heat transferred from the fingers to the bristles of the brush to the canvas. I could change all that, I thought. I could warm him up and make him a better artist.

⁓

Strangely enough, when Gabriel and I got into bed that night his hands felt too hot on my body. They made me sweaty and uncomfortable, which he mistook for passion. I found myself imagining how the cold, cold hands of Michael Bon Chance would feel instead. I tried to push the thought out of my mind but it was as if he had formed an icicle with his touch that had pierced my skin and was now melting and spreading out inside of my body.

"Are you happy here," Gabriel asked, "spending so much time by yourself?"

"I had an interesting day today," I began. "I wasn't by myself at all."

But Gabriel was asleep before I could finish, and I never got to tell him the tales of Michael, or Levon and his bedridden mother and her ceramic finger with its real red nail.

35

Gabriel woke up at eight the next morning and as I heard him shower and watched him dress, doing all the things which made him so familiar to me, I regretted my decision to meet Michael.

"Do you have to leave for school so early?" I asked. "Stay and I'll cook you breakfast."

"I can't today. My class is going to meet in the library and if I don't study I'll be way behind."

I put my arms around him and held him tight.

"Hey, hey," he said, "I'll be home tonight and we'll have dinner together, and maybe take a walk or see a movie. Okay?"

He kissed me goodbye and my choice became clear. I could spend another day alone on the balcony drinking coffee and watching the wisteria grow, or I could go visit Michael and have another human being to talk to.

I lay down in bed to get more sleep, but Levon was at my door by 10:00.

"Did you drop the finger at the chapel?" he asked.

"What happened to *Good morning, neighbor*?" I said.

He smiled with his head tilted to the side.

"Good morning, Miss Evangeline. Did you drop off the finger?"

"Yes. It's on the table in the front, next to the two-headed doll."

"I'm gonna check it out, you know."

"I'm sure you are."

"I gotta make sure my mama stays well."

"Is she still in bed?"

"No, she's already up. It's been a good morning for her so I had a feeling you did right by the digit. Thank you."

"You're welcome."

"You look pretty today. Are you going to see your new boyfriend?"

"What are you talking about? I don't have a new boyfriend."

"Really? Cause my mama gets that same look on her face when there's a new man coming to the house for dinner."

"What look?"

"That dreamy face."

"I just woke up from dreaming, that's why I look like that. I'm going to see a friend, that's all."

"What's your friend's name?"

"Michael."

"Michael and Evangeline sittin' in a tree, k-i-s-s-i-n-g."

He smiled again with straight white teeth and a few missing that didn't mar his teenaged beauty one bit.

"Aren't you a little old for that song?" I asked.

"Does your boyfriend know about your friend Michael?"

"He does."

"Don't worry. Even if he didn't, I would never tell him. I'm not the gossiping type."

"Don't you go to school?"

"I told you, I'm taking a year off to take care of my mama. She's real sick and I'm all she has besides my grandma, who's old and lives all the way down on the bayou anyhow."

"Does your grandma ever come up here and help you out?"

"Nah. She lives pretty far away. Did you ever hear that song 'Down on the Bayou Chère'?"

Levon snapped his fingers in tune to a song that was playing in his head.

"Nope. I never heard that one," I said.

"It's real famous and it was written in the town where she lives. I'll play it for you someday. I have it on a record. Vinyl."

"Can you sing it?"

"I can't sing that one but I know another one you might like. It goes like this: *'Ta femme est partie. Ta maison elle a pris en feu.'*"

Levon's changing voice was scratchy and plaintive.

"Pretty," I said. "What does it mean?"

"It means your woman is gone and your house is on fire."

"Nice sentiment."

"Your house is on fire means your relationship is over. Cajuns talk about marriage like it's a house. My old grandma taught me that one. We used to go down and see her every weekend. She'd drive us into town to hear bands play or we'd go to the theater and watch a show. She'd always look at me afterward and say, Levon, remember; it's the singer, not the song."

"Maybe so."

"Hey Evangeline, how come you never invite me into your house? How come I gotta stand out here in the hall like a stranger?"

I exhaled.

"Because I'm being very rude. I'm sorry, Levon. I'm in a bit of a rush today, so how about next time we sit down and have some iced tea and talk."

"That's more like it."

"Does your mother know you come over here and talk to me?"

"My mama knows everything."

36

Michael's house was on Magazine Street across from a little diner called Johnny River. It was a local, homemade-looking place with a screen door and dishes that didn't match. The kind of place tourists never find unless they're visiting a friend in New Orleans who happens to live in the neighborhood.

The eggs came three on a plate, over easy but still hot in the center, perfectly done, with two biscuits, gravy, sausage, grits, and hot sauce on the side, and because of them I liked Michael just a little bit more after breakfast than I had before.

I walked across the street listening to the screen door slam behind me. His house was the second in from the corner. A narrow Victorian painted lilac on the outside with cream-colored steps, chipped and sunken in the middle from who knows how many years and how many footsteps.

Michael appeared in the doorway while my fist was still up in the air, before I had the chance to knock.

"Evangeline," he said. "I'm so glad you came."

He was wearing an antique blue silk smoking jacket and jeans. His smooth chest showed through the open jacket, making him seem dressed and undressed at the same time.

I walked up a flight of stairs and followed him through a dark, narrow hallway. He walked ahead of me under a wooden arch and into the living room, but I stopped short in the entranceway, startled by the unexpected and sheer beauty of his home.

"Come on in," he said, walking backward, beckoning with his fingers and fading into the room.

I stood under the arch and absorbed the image.

Rose and blue and ancient oriental rugs held pale pink loveseats with curved arms and perfectly faded silk upholstery. Sheer white-winged angels floated on a ceiling of baby-blue sky with clouds of spun gold. And eastern-facing windows of blue stained glass held paler blue stained-glass crosses in the middle. Daylight and streetlamps were obliterated by thick velvet curtains with gold tasseled ropes, and a small, dusty beam of faded light managed to seep past the heavy drapes, making it look like the tail end of the day instead of the early part of the afternoon.

His home was lavish and seductive, and I thought it rare that a man living alone could create a thing of such intensity. For the second time in two days I found myself having to adjust my opinion of Michael Bon Chance.

It was a marble fountain that ended my reverie and brought me back down to earth. It was the true centerpiece of the room, with water slowly seeping from a cracked jug and dripping over a statue of a nude couple, bathing. I cringed at the sound.

Michael looked at me.

"Something wrong?"

"It's the dripping."

He went over to the bar and poured me a glass of wine.

"You're tense. Maybe this will help."

I took a sip from the glass and put it down on the fireplace mantel. I caught a glimpse of Michael and myself in the mirror above the fire and felt trapped by how beautiful we looked in the rose glow of the dragon's-head lamps with pale pink bulbs. I stepped away from him and reminded myself that it was the lighting and not anything inherent in the two of us. I shook my head back and forth as if to remind myself that there was no two of us.

"Come, let me show you the rest of the house," he said. "There are no more fountains, I promise."

I followed him through the kitchen and past the bedroom. He did not offer to show me where he slept, which put me at ease, but I couldn't help glancing inside anyway. I caught sight of a burgundy bedspread embroidered with a large gold cross and a marble headboard with a carved pastel Madonna in the center.

It was a long, railroad-style house, and as we passed the bedroom we continued on walking straight through to the back.

"Here's where we'll be working," Michael said. "My favorite place in the world. My painting studio."

Looking around the room I understood why Gabriel could not describe it and why he wanted me to see it for myself. Larger than the living and dining rooms together, it was less of a painting studio and more of a painting hall.

The walls were a deep sea blue with images of swirling water and high waves. Unsteady, I reached back for something to hold on to, and Michael was there.

Mermaids rose out of the seascape with water up to their naked breasts. They held their long, thin arms out toward a full, yellow moon, and their endless hair, like strands of seaweed, trailed over their bodies.

On the ceiling was an ocean of blue, making me feel like I was underwater, submerged with Michael and his mermaids.

On one side of the room was a bookcase, which overflowed with dusty tomes. On closer look the books were on the same topic as the walls—nymphs, water spirits, mermaids, and bird people. Titles like *Incantations of Circe*, *Nymphs in Greek Mythology*, and Ovid's *Metamorphoses* caught my eye.

"Have you heard of the sirens' song?" he asked. "Bird women

of the depths who lure men to a watery death with their beautiful songs and then feast on their souls. Women with unique powers. Impossible for men to resist."

He came around and stood in front of me.

"Everyone I paint is my siren song for as long as they're sitting," he said. "Today, that person is you, but only until the painting is done." He smiled. "So don't get used to it."

I turned away so that he would not see that I was getting used to it already.

I focused my eyes away from him and on the smaller details. There were crosses everywhere. Tiny ones in unexpected places. Hard to see. Nailed under antique dressers that held half-empty tubes of paint in every color; dangling from chains that pulled down to turn on lights; doubling as doorknobs and drawer handles. In one corner of the room there was a wooden statue taller than myself with the face of a young girl and the body of an old woman whose bony hands held an antique cross and rosary beads.

The center of the room was lined with church pews.

"These are where you'll be lying when I paint you," he said. "Go ahead, try each one until you get a sense of it and then let me know which one you like best. Spend as much time with them as you like. Sitting is harder than it looks and I want you to be as comfortable as possible. Run your hands along the length of the wood and feel the indentations. Notice the color. The scent. But don't take too long," he said, "you won't be alive forever. One day we'll both be like these church pews. Stiff and motionless."

"Are you going to paint me today?"

"That's why you came here, isn't it?"

"I want this portrait for Gabriel, as a gift."

Michael came over and put his arm around my waist. It was as cool as seawater.

"I want to paint you because you want me to. That's the only way it works. Portrait painting is an intimate relationship where we both understand the project and we both give it our all. Do you understand? This is something that takes place between the two of us."

"I understand."

"Good. Then let's have a toast to our mutual endeavor."

He picked up a bottle from the floor next to his easel.

"Bourbon," he said. "The drink of sailors and sea nymphs. The very same drink we had when we first met at the Broken Heart Ballroom."

"I don't remember."

"I do. I remember everything about you. Every single detail. Even the things you can't remember, yourself."

"It's too early for bourbon," I said.

"It's not a second too soon," he answered.

Michael drank straight from the bottle and then handed it to me. I drank one mouthful, and then another, straightaway. After the third or fourth I felt as if the two of us were lost at sea and I could tell him anything at all because we were the last two people either of us would ever lay eyes on.

"My grandmother died just a little while ago," I said. "I don't get along with my mother very well, but I loved my grandmother more than anyone."

Michael lay down on the pew next to mine with the bottle in his hand. He crossed his legs at the ankles.

"Well, a grandmother is just a mother with a lot more practice," he said. "Like a mother with a second chance."

I smiled. I had never thought about it that way and for a moment he made me like my own mother a little bit more.

"You would have enjoyed my grandmother's company," I said. "She didn't care what other people thought; she did whatever she wanted. I can tell that you're the same kind of person."

"Was Gabriel at her funeral?" he asked.

"No, he was working that day."

"That's too bad, he must feel terrible about missing it."

I reached over and took the bottle out of Michael's hand and thought about how Gabriel had never once expressed sadness at having missed Louise's funeral.

"Promise me you'll never talk about Louise," I said. "I don't know why I told you about her."

"I'm just a painter and you're just a girl who lost her grand-mother, her favorite person in the whole world. I understand that, I do. It was the bourbon talking, not you. I'll never mention her to another living soul."

I sat upright and watched the mermaids spin around me.

"I have to go now. Gabriel's waiting for me."

"Gabriel is in the library studying, where he'll be for the next several years. I'm offering you friendship, Evangeline, that's all. Don't be afraid of me. I need a friend as much as you do."

"I suppose you do."

"At least let me give you a hug before you leave."

Michael put his arms around me and I could feel the smooth skin of his chest through the opening in the silk robe. He buried his face in my hair, underneath, at the nape of my neck where my scent was strongest. But unlike anyone else who had ever rested their face in that spot, he did not inhale deeply, and he not seem to take any pleasure in my scent, and so I did not pull away.

37

Gabriel and I walked along the bank of the Mississippi River in the dark. The waterway felt cool after another humid Louisiana day spent somewhere in the high nineties. I asked him what he'd studied that day at school and he pulled my hair back and whispered in my ear, "blood," and in that moment I didn't know which was worse, red and white cells, or paint of the same colors.

"What does it smell like?" I asked.

"Warm and inviting but strong, like iron."

He turned my arm so that the inside was facing up and he traced the thin, branching veins on my wrist with his fingertips.

"See how blue they are? That's blood you're looking at. It's the color of blood through the skin."

I thought about Michael's deep blue studio and wondered whether his beautiful seascape was really an ocean of blood.

Gabriel and I began walking again, hand in hand, along the quay, watching the giant freighters moving down the river in slow motion.

"I've made the decision to specialize in hematology," he said, "but it means another two years at Tulane. Do you think you could live here with me, in New Orleans, for that long?"

I was quiet. I didn't tell him that I felt a constant tension here, like a rain that refused to fall.

"Tell me about blood and why you love it so much. I need to know why you want to spend so much time with it, instead of me."

"Some doctors think blood type says a lot about the personality," he said. "Type A is calm and trustworthy, and B is creative and excitable. The Japanese ask the question *What's your blood type* as often as Americans ask *What's your sign.*"

"I bet you're type A," I said.

"I'm O. The universal donor."

"Of course you are. The one that everybody loves."

"Do you know yours?" he asked.

"I don't."

"Well, I think it must be the most rare."

We kissed on the quay on the bank of the Mississippi and the day with Michael faded into the muddy water and washed away.

"You look different," Gabriel said. "So serious. I'm sorry we haven't been able to spend more time together. It must be hard to be alone every day."

"I'm not alone all the time. I saw Michael today."

I had thought about not telling him. I didn't want it to prey on his mind while he had so much work to do at school, but now that it was out in the open I felt better.

"He asked me to sit for a portrait. It was that night when we were at the Broken Heart Ballroom, and I said yes."

Gabriel dropped my hand and sat down on a bench at the water's edge. I secretly hoped that he would get angry enough to do the hard work of persuading me not to go back to the house on Magazine Street.

"Why didn't you tell me until now?"

"I tried to, the other night after the cemetery, but you fell asleep."

"So, at first you didn't like him at all and now he's your future plan? Now he's your reason for staying in New Orleans? Maybe you *should* go home."

"Don't exaggerate, Gabriel. It's just something to do while you're at school. It's like having a job."

"It's not a job unless there's a paycheck with your name on it at the end of the week."

"I went to see the studio, that's all. Nothing's happened. He hasn't even begun the painting."

Gabriel stopped and faced me. He tucked my hair behind my ears.

"I trust you, but I need to know that I can focus on medicine and not worry that you'll get bored, or lonely, and end up leaving me. A lot of relationships end during medical school. It's common. The other person is alone too much and ends up meeting someone else."

"You really think about things like that? About me being lonely?"

"Of course I do. All the time. I don't want to lose you, Evangeline."

I put my arms around Gabriel and with my chin resting on his shoulder I spotted a dog-walker in the distance. He had so many dogs that he looked more like a shepherd with a flock of sheep. I chose to focus on him instead of my loneliness, Gabriel's fear of losing me, or Michael's ability to pull on my thoughts.

I could have that job, I thought to myself. If I wanted to I could walk dogs and make new friends in the park that didn't live anywhere near Magazine Street. In fact, I knew enough about them that as they approached I could make out two golden retrievers, a black lab, a gray-and-white terrier, two miniature greyhounds, and a German shepherd.

From my comfortable distance in Gabriel's arms I watched as the dogs barked and pulled on their leashes. The closer they got the less the walker was able to keep them in line. I was perfectly aware that it was my scent, so easy to detect in the hot Louisiana nighttime, that was agitating them, but I stood still and did not move away, using their barking and pulling as a distraction from the conversation about Michael and sitting for the painting.

As the dogs came near I saw that they were well kept and neatly groomed. They were in prime condition, muscular and excited, and pretty quickly their strength was too much for the walker to handle. I watched, fascinated, while Gabriel tried to pull me away. I watched while the walker called the dogs by name, yelling at them and pulling back on their leashes as hard as he could. I watched while he grabbed the black lab by the collar with his free hand, but I knew as a single individual there was not much that he could do and the moment would come when the dogs would win the struggle.

In no time at all the three largest animals broke free and ran right at me. At that point I did try to make a run for it, but they were too close and they overtook me, knocking me to the ground.

I wasn't exactly afraid, because they seemed to like me, but Gabriel was another story. He tried to pull them off me but they didn't take to him at all. They threatened him with their teeth, snarling and growling at him and then turning right around and licking and pawing at my skin. I let them do it too. I let them lick away the memory of the lilac exterior, the dripping fountain, the painting studio, the mermaids, and the smooth skin of Michael's chest under the silk smoking jacket. I let them go on and on until they licked away the entire house and even the diner across the street.

The walker, who until that moment seemed to be in some kind of suspended animation, watching the scene unfold, finally let go of the remaining two dogs and ran toward us. He grabbed the distracted animals by their collars and was finally able to pull them away and herd them off.

"I'm so sorry about this," he said. "Nothing like it has ever happened before."

The dogs continued to snarl at Gabriel and salivate at me as the man picked up the leashes and held them tight.

"I'm fine," I said. "Really, it wasn't so bad."

Gabriel and the walker were both breathing heavily from containing the dogs while I was lying on the grass, leaning on my elbows, wishing I were still surrounded by soft, warm bodies and wagging tails. It was as if we'd had two separate but simultaneous experiences. As if Gabriel and the walker were separated from me by that thin cellophane lining that I had first noticed when I met Rayanne back in Cyril.

"You weren't scared?" Gabriel asked.

"Not a bit."

"Does Michael have a dog?"

"I don't think so."

He didn't say anything, but he looked relieved, as if Michael having a dog would somehow draw me back to the lilac Victorian.

We walked in silence toward Canal Street on our way to the ferry. We had planned to take the free ride to Algiers and back. At that moment all I wanted to do was close my eyes, smell the water from the Mississippi, and feel the wind plastering my hair against my head.

Holding Gabriel's hand I worried that it wasn't just Michael, but New Orleans itself that was coming between us. I had never felt a city with so much pull before, so much personality, so much input into my thoughts and relationships.

38

The next morning I woke up with a new resolve. There were many things to do in New Orleans and many people to meet. I could certainly figure out how to entertain myself without the company of Michael Bon Chance.

Despite the heat I got out of bed with vigor and surveyed myself in the bathroom mirror. The scent had become such a focal point of my life that I'd forgotten what I looked like as just a human form without my new and incredible vaporish presence. I would say that in an odd way the scent had made me invisible. I could have looked like anything at all, worn any clothes I wanted to, ill fitting or not, bright purple or bland beige—none of it would have mattered in the least, as those were no longer the things that people noticed when I was by their side.

But standing there in front of the mirror without an audience to validate the beauty of my skin through its scent, it was clear to me that my body had gotten into a bit of trouble. I could see that all of the incredibly rich foods of New Orleans, the fried chicken, the bread pudding, the catfish po'boys, had, in this short span of time, made me larger. My clothes were tight and uncomfortable. I was robust, almost curvy. A body type I had never even come close to. I felt sexy and attractive and cumbersome and unattractive at the same time, but at least I had an answer to the question of how I would spend my day.

While I was not much for exercise, the hotel down the block offered a gym with a steam room and sauna thrown in for free. I would take the time to relax and maybe strike up a conversation with a person who was over fourteen years old and did not live across the hall from me or across the street from Johnny River's diner.

Peeking through the window of the hotel into the gym I had the sudden urge to go straight back to bed. I was tired all over again looking at the endless rows of sleek machines and all of the people using them. Up and down they went on the stair climbers, or running to nowhere on the treadmills, sweat pouring down their bodies like the cherubs in the fountain in Michael's living room, like the new Sisyphuses of our time.

Inside I found myself repulsed by the physical exertion around me. I had to hold myself back from the juice bar with its fruity drinks and protein bars and with great difficulty I closed off my desire for food and headed for the steam room. I figured that if I sat long enough I could sweat out the touch of Michael Bon Chance's smooth chest and long, cold fingers.

I had chosen the middle of the day, hoping that most of the hotel guests were lined up for a ghost tour of New Orleans or buying pictures of Marie Laveau, the voodoo queen, and the other gym members, the ones who actually lived in the area, would be at work.

It was a good choice and the locker room was empty. I stripped naked, wrapped myself in a plush towel, and entered the steam room.

I sat on a cedar bench with my head against the tiles of the back wall. I closed my eyes against the heat and vapor and Louise immediately appeared in my mind. I could hear her telling me that a good scent would make a person irresistible to everyone around them; that it should make people feel intimate toward someone they did not know, and in fact had never seen before. It would draw people in, she said, in an animal sort of way.

Louise's own dusky, sexual scent rose up in my nose as I studied her image in my mind. She seemed to be pushing her chin out in front of her as if she were pointing to a future that I was yet unable to see.

The murmur of soft voices woke me out of my reverie and I found myself surrounded by women in an incredible variety of shades and sizes. I had no idea where they'd come from, as the steam had been empty just moments before, and I wondered how long my eyes had been closed.

The legs of a beautiful brunette were touching my own. She

looked into my eyes and then draped her calves over my thighs. I let her do it. I knew she couldn't help it and did not understand it herself.

My own pores had taken over the cedar-and-lavender infusion that the gym pumped into the steam room. It was now filled with hot, dusky jasmine, red velvet rose, and naked women, their own personal scents slightly altering my own, but that detail was probably only noticeable to me.

The women were crowding in and pressing together. The space so full that some of them were forced to stay outside with their faces pressed against the glass, waiting for an opening to arise so they could slip themselves inside.

The air was limited and claustrophobia pervasive. It worked on me and I had to get out, even though I knew that leaving the room would require that I be touched all over, by everybody.

I stood up as abruptly as I could in order to clear just the smallest amount of space that would allow me a bit of movement and I pushed forward. I slithered through the bodies, oily smooth from various lotions and skin creams and even sweat itself; it was like moving through a room of the utmost slippery softness and all at once I could understand the unending infatuation men had for the female body.

Outside the door I sat down in front of my locker and allowed the stream of women behind me to touch my hair and back, to massage my feet and shoulders. I didn't belong to myself anymore; the power of my scent had made me public property.

As I sat there being pampered and petted, touched and stroked, I thought about how I should be able to enjoy all the love and attention being showered on me as if I were a rock star on tour, but instead I felt more isolated than I ever had. They loved something that was not a true part of myself, something that came out of a tiny glass jar, and I was sure they would all run away if I dared to break the spell by uttering even one single word.

It was as if the gift of being seen and adored, which people strive for their entire lives, which is the raison d'être of so many, was being wasted on me, someone who would have been more than satisfied with one or two friends to spend an afternoon.

In moments such as this I had to wonder why Louise had given me such a public gift. And I had to acknowledge, although I hated to think of her in any other way than magnificent, that the longer I had this present from her, the lonelier my life had become, making Michael Bon Chance all the more necessary to my day-to-day happiness.

39

The next day I was out of bed as soon as Gabriel was on the other side of the front door. I would go back to the house on Magazine Street. Of course I would. I would go back to the only person in New Orleans, or maybe anywhere, who seemed to like me for me.

It was raining outside, which was not a good sign. I looked out the window and told myself that I would do as Father Madrid had suggested and hop between the drops.

The thick Louisiana summertime humidity had already seeped into the house, making my mind moody and my hair puffy. I didn't want Michael to paint me like this. My first portrait would not be titled *Girl with Frizzy Hair.*

I stared at my face under the fluorescent light of the bathroom mirror until all I could see were the imperfections, the tiny lines on the sides of my eyes, and the slightly red blotches around my nose. I looked like I had a cold. Was it the bathroom lighting, the dampness of New Orleans, or was I getting sick, or old? I piled on foundation until my face was one solid color, all shadows and redness gone from sight. For one brief moment that should have been much longer I wondered why I cared so much about what I looked like before seeing Michael Bon Chance.

I got dressed in a hurry but not so much of a hurry that I wasn't careful what I wore. I chose a nude-colored body suit, the same cream-colored skirt that was really a vintage piece of lingerie that I'd worn when I first met Michael at the Broken Heart Ballroom, and gold sandals.

I was locking the door when I spotted Levon sitting in the middle of the stairwell. He stared up at me with a face that said I wasn't going to get past him without a little bit of conversation.

"Why are you all dressed up and covered in makeup?" he asked.

"I'm not covered in makeup."

"Yes you are, and it's first thing in the morning. I can only imagine what you look like when you go out at night."

"Well, keep your imagination to yourself. Are you locked out of your house?"

"No. I got the key right here."

He held up a New Orleans Saints keychain.

"Are you going to see your friend Michael?"

"Yes, in fact, I am."

He swung his keychain back and forth like a pendulum, as if he were trying to hypnotize me out of my plan.

"Is it because you're afraid he can't see you?"

"What do you mean?"

"My mama says that a man who sees you is better than a man who loves you. But if you're lucky, they're the same. I don't know what that means, but maybe you do."

"I don't know what it means either."

"You look nicer without all that stuff on your face."

"Thanks, Levon. That's sweet."

"I may be young, but I know what beauty is, and that ain't it."

I looked at him long and hard, staring right into those black eyes set against the blond hair and bronze skin. If anyone knew about beauty it would be a kid born with so very much of it.

"You stay here," I said. "I'll be right back."

I went back into my apartment and washed my face. I was still close enough to Levon's age to know that kids really do know everything.

"Better?" I asked, back at the stairwell.

"Much. You're a real beauty when you leave yourself alone."

"Thanks, Levon."

"No problem. You know your boyfriend passed right by me this morning without saying a word. He didn't even see me sitting here."

"He's in medical school. His mind is occupied."

"What's he studying?"

"Blood."

"I saw that tattoo on his arm."

"It's a birthmark."

"It's a sign."

"Of what?"

"I don't know, but a birthmark like that is a sure sign of something. It's a star, so maybe he's from another galaxy."

"Levon, why are you sitting here all by yourself? Is your mother home?"

"My mama's a fortune teller. She works at night and sleeps in the day."

"Does she work in the scent shop on St. Philip Street?"

"No, she works right here at home; her customers come in at night after I'm asleep."

"So you're alone all day long?"

"She's sleeping, so I can come and go as I please. I like it that way."

"What are you thinking about when you're sitting on these steps all morning?"

"It's hard to say. My mind's fixed on hidden interests."

"Like what?"

"Things I can't talk about. It's not that I don't want to, but I can't."

"Why not?"

"I don't know. Things want to stay inside my head. They don't want to come out."

"What if you tried to push them out?"

Levon shook his head.

"It's not a matter of trying, Evangeline."

"What's it a matter of, then?"

"There's a big windstorm between me and everybody else. Big, swirly, curly winds. I can see them clear as day sitting between me and other people. They'd take my words and blow them all to bits if I tried to get them out."

I wondered about Levon. It was as if the big, swirly winds just blew him away, and blew him *my* way. Walking to Michael's I was thankful for him. Without our chat I would have gotten there way too early, looking like a made-up fool. Good thing the curly winds didn't blow his words away on this particular morning.

40

All along the way to Magazine Street I had a strange feeling. Maybe Levon blew it there with his winds, maybe not, but I had the feeling that I'd turned a corner somewhere, and it happened even before I met Michael.

Ever since I stepped off that plane onto Louisiana soil, I'd been plagued with the same feeling. Every day, every moment I'd spent in New Orleans seemed somehow out of step with where my life was supposed to be. I felt as if I were on a journey without an end, as if I were being blown forward and I couldn't turn around because the wind at my back was too strong.

Maybe it hadn't started in New Orleans at all. Maybe it began in Cyril. All I knew was I had a feeling deep in my bones that I was marching to a tune that was already laid out for me. All the notes and chords, the minor and major lifts, were already known by someone, somewhere, just not by me.

It was hot again and humid as rain but without the drops. I kept putting one foot in front of the other but my mind lagged behind, waiting for the thunder and lightning.

Finally the lilac Victorian was in sight, its exterior so calm, midway between a happy sky blue and a mysterious purple.

I stopped in front before going in. I looked up at the second-floor balcony for some sign of movement in the studio, but there was none, so instead, I went across the street to Johnny River's for a cup of coffee. If Michael hadn't spotted me outside his house, if I didn't have the psychic pull to force him out of whatever it was that he was doing that morning, then I knew that it wasn't time for us just yet.

I sat at the counter, not wanting to take up an entire table for myself. A girl with purple streaks in her hair and black horn-rimmed glasses, a different waitress than I'd had the first time, came by to take my order. I could tell that she could tell that I was from out of town, and she seemed annoyed.

"What can I get for you?" she asked without looking at me, as if I were a moment in her morning that she could not process.

"A coffee, please."

"Right."

She returned with the coffee and put it down in front of me, black.

"Excuse me," I said, "can I have some cream, a teaspoon, a napkin, and maybe a glass of water?"

She sighed under the strain of my request and put the items on the counter without saying a word, which made me think fondly on the perfection of Rayanne's service back at the diner in Cyril.

I wanted to ask her about the man across the street in the lilac house. I figured she would know much more about him than either Gabriel, myself, or even Levon, who seemed to know everything about everything, even if he could not quite get it out of his mouth, but she'd already made it clear that she would never help me in any way even if I caught fire right there at the counter.

A couple came in and sat down next to me. Definitely locals—I could tell by the way the waitress greeted them. Nicely.

The girl had four or five tiny braids woven into her straight red hair and the man was thin, with skin-tight black pants and a slightly dirty off-white wife-beater. He had a silver ring on every finger. Skulls, knots, spikes, evil eyes, plain bands, you name it, he wore it.

I stared at his hand, hoping he would talk about the rings, and when that didn't work I went the more common route.

"Pass the sugar?" I said.

"What?"

"Can you pass the sugar?"

"Oh yeah, course," said the guy with the rings, in a British accent that sounded put on.

"You from around here?" I asked.

"Well, yeah," he said, which I took as an admission of his fake accent.

"I'm from New York," I said.

"Cool."

"This is a great place."

"It is."

I let the conversation go on and on in this most painful trajectory, how are you, nice town, hot weather, that sort of thing, until I felt I had gained enough traction to ask about Michael, but as it turned out I did not have to work nearly so hard because the girl with the tiny braids ended up doing the job for me. Maybe she didn't like that I was talking to her boyfriend or maybe she was just bored. Either way, she was a gold mine when it came to Michael.

"Are you here alone?" she asked.

"I'm waiting for a friend, someone I met in the Quarter," I said. "He lives across the street in that purple Victorian house. His name is Michael Bon Chance. Do you know him?"

"Not really, but I've seen him around," said the girl.

"Where?" asked the guy with obvious jealousy that I needed to stop in its tracks if I wanted to get any information from his girlfriend.

"In the park," she said. "He's that portrait painter—you know him, silly."

"Oh yeah. The guy with the silk smoking jackets," he said with a slight eye roll.

"I have a friend who has a friend who dated him once," said the girl.

"Yes?"

"That's right. I heard that after spending a few months with him she was never the same again."

"How so?" I asked.

"Well"—she leaned in close to me like people do when the story is about to get really good—"I heard that she fell in love with him right away. As soon as she saw him."

"And?"

"And it was a terrible idea because he made believe he loved her deeply even though he never did. He spent every minute of every day with her and then when he was sure she loved him, he walked away and never spoke to her again. Wouldn't even take a phone call. No explanation. Not a single word. Supposedly she fell to pieces and had to be sent to an institution. A mental institution," she whispered.

I studied the girl, trying to decipher the accuracy of her story. I looked for clues to her honesty in the look in her eyes, and for signs of her intelligence in the sound of her voice. I couldn't find either. And anyway I could not imagine Michael, so involved with his own work, actually taking the time to make believe that he had fallen in love with a woman he'd just met.

"She was probably a lonely person who made up the whole relationship in her mind. It happens all the time," I said, not knowing a single person who it had ever actually happened to, and then having to question my own level of honesty.

"Oh no. You've got it all wrong," said the girl. "She wasn't a lonely woman. She was a busy doctor. A psychiatrist doctor."

I took a good, long sip of Johnny River's chicory-flavored coffee, wishing that it included a shot of bourbon. The girl with the tiny braids had delivered an unexpected answer that I had to give myself a moment to consider

"Is she okay now?" I asked. "The psychiatrist?"

"I heard she got through it all right, but she spends most of her days in church now, praying. I don't know her firsthand or anything like that, so don't take my word on it, but I heard that she never practiced again after it was all over between them and she had a real hard time paying back her bills from medical school."

"I see."

"Why are you so interested?" she asked.

"I was thinking of buying a painting from him."

She shrugged her shoulders. "I wouldn't, but do what you want. You're just visiting, so he probably can't get to you anyhow."

She turned her back toward me and began talking to her boyfriend in hushed tones, no doubt continuing the conversation about Michael in more detail than they would ever give to an outsider.

I asked the waitress for the check and she took her sweet time bringing it to the counter. In the meantime I tried to listen in on the conversation next to me, with no luck. The girl had the lowest voice I'd ever heard. The thin guy must have had some supersonic hearing. Neither of them had any sense of smell as far as I could tell, as they did not seem to notice me at all. They were a perfect couple and I felt like telling them they should try to stay together forever and not let petty things get in their way, but what was the point? They wouldn't listen to me anyway, and who was I to give them advice now that I had let an entire city and its portrait painter come between Gabriel and me? Now, bring Levon into the picture, let him tell them a thing or two, and maybe they really would stay together.

41

The bell jangled on the screen door of the diner as I walked out. The summer air was murky and heavy and smelled like roses and lavender. I heard a tune from Aaron Neville floating out of someone's window on the other end of the street. I could tell it was him from the trembling, angelic quality of the voice. I'm no music connoisseur, but once you hear something like that you never forget it.

That was the thing about New Orleans. Even in the morning, with the city all quiet like it was now, you could do something as simple as turning a corner and you might find someone weeping, or someone singing, or praying, or laughing hysterically, or harming or charming someone else. It took getting used to. There was a lot happening all over in unexpected places and the experience was bringing me closer to Louise. I could see how she grew up loving the smell of things. She wasn't really all that strange, she was just from Louisiana. And even worse, she was from Fayetteville, where I had yet to go. Who knew what I would find there?

That's how New Orleans was for me, like a dream I couldn't gain control over, with stories coming from everywhere that just kept moving forward and changing. There was no backtracking, no thinking things over, only movement that was slow and dreamy but forward nonetheless.

In fact, that one small amount of space between the diner and the lilac Victorian was so absolutely absorbing that in the short time it took me to get across the street I'd already forgotten about the psychiatrist whose life had been ruined by Michael Bon Chance.

I knocked on the door and he opened it right away, as if he had been standing there behind it waiting for the sound of my hand on his house.

"You came," he said. "I'm glad."

I did not need to tell him that I'd already put my makeup on, washed it off, and sat in Johnny River's for an hour before crossing the street.

"You look frozen, Evangeline. You're as tense as a wax figure."

You should have seen me earlier, I thought.

"This isn't such an easy place to come to," I said.

"Why not? I've been more than hospitable, haven't I?"

"Hospitable" sounded like "hospital," which reminded me of "mental hospital" and the woman he may or may not have dated and then destroyed with his fake love.

"Are you going to invite me in?"

"I'm not sure. You're almost too rigid to paint. That is the reason you came here, to sit for me. Correct?"

I felt my face turn pink, wondering whether or not I had come to sit for the painting or simply to be with Michael.

I stood there not knowing what to do. I hadn't planned on it being he who changed his mind. If he didn't want to paint I could go back to the apartment on St. Louis and talk to Levon. Maybe walk through the streets of the Quarter like a ghost. Or hang out in Jackson Square and learn how to read the tarot cards. So far every conversation I'd had this morning made me want to slide back under the sheets and stay there.

"Come on in, Evangeline. Of course I want to paint you," he said. "Who wouldn't want to paint you?"

And with that I stepped through the doorway into Michael's watery world.

We walked into the main living area before going into the studio and I sat on the antique loveseat. I draped my arm over the armrest, hoping to look relaxed. I didn't know why I was so tight, but I tried not to think about it and I just let my nerves sway in the wind, unchecked.

"I'm glad you're nervous around me," Michael said. "It means that we have something to show each other, to teach each other. It means that we were not meant to be simply friends but something far more interesting and enlightening. To be honest, I feel the same way around you."

I got off the loveseat and started walking toward the back of the house ahead of Michael.

"I'm ready to get started now," I said.

42

On the floor of the studio was an inlaid pentagram that I hadn't noticed the day before.

"I like the design, that's all," said Michael. "Its perfect symmetry interests me, not its occult meanings, if that's what you're worried about. Although I have to admit I enjoy watching the fear in others when they see it."

He laughed and the sound of him made me feel impaled on a point of the pentagram.

"Why do you want people to be uncomfortable?" I asked.

"Why do you want people to be comfortable?" he countered. "Discomfort is the arena of learning."

Michael went over to the bookshelf and pulled down a large book with the title *Famous Nudes*. He sat down next to me on a pew, opened the book, and spread it across both of our laps.

"These are some of the most beautiful and famous paintings ever made. I've been studying them for days, looking for ideas on how best to work with you."

He turned the pages.

Nude Woman on a Bed and *Nude Woman Reclining* by Van Gogh. *Nude Egyptian Girl* by John Singer Sargent. *Female Nude Study* by Gustav Klimt. *The Water Nymph* by John Maler Collier. *Benefits Supervisor Sleeping* by Lucien Freud. The great nudes of Picasso, *Girl in a Chemise, Les Demoiselles d'Avignon, Female Nude and Smoker,* and several by Modigliani.

"Which is your favorite?" he asked.

I liked *The Water Nymph*. It was a dark-haired woman sitting in a dimly lit deep green forest on a gray stone slab overlooking a dark blue spring. It was a contemplative, moody piece and the girl looked the way I imagined I would if I were alone and someone was staring at me without my knowing that they were there.

"I can paint you like that. I can make you look just like the girl in the picture."

He lifted the book off our laps and turned toward me.

"We would cover you up like this."

He took my hair in both of his hands and brought it around to the front of my body on either side.

"What are you covering?"

"Your breasts."

"You mean you want me to pose nude?"

"Yes, of course. You want to look like the girl in the painting, don't you? The water nymph is always nude."

It hadn't occurred to me that he would want that.

"Look at yourself."

I looked down at my hands in my lap.

"Not there. Look at your clothes. You're wearing a top the same color as your skin. Somewhere inside of yourself you were already thinking about being naked, only you didn't know it yet. You're almost there, Evangeline. All you have to do is think like an artist and see your body as a painting instead of a body, which is how I see it."

I looked back through the pages of the nudes in the book. I thought about how all of those beautiful women had agreed to pose without their clothes for the sake of the work, or the love of the artist. I played with the straps of my bodysuit, sliding them off my shoulders and then back again while Michael stared at the mark the vial had left on my neck. The minutes ticked off one by one. The sound of the clock like water dripping somewhere in the distance.

"I can't do it."

"Not yet," he said.

"Can't you use your imagination?"

Michael got off the pew, kneeled down in front of me, and once again he arranged my hair, draping it over my breasts, smoothing it out so that I looked as much like the water nymph as possible.

"I will if I have to," he said, "but I wish I didn't."

He was careful not to touch my body, only my hair, and he closed his eyes whenever he came close to me in what I thought was an attempt at maintaining some sense of privacy between us. I believed it took a lot for him to stay at a distance, minimal as it was, and I was grateful for his self-control.

And then, just as I was getting used to his presence and the feel of his hands in my hair, trusting in the process of the painter and his muse, he put his arms around me, drew me close to him, and whispered in my ear, "I think God himself created this scent just for you, Evangeline."

So sure had I been that it was not the red liquid that had drawn him to me, so badly had I wanted him to be attracted to me and not my scent, that his words were a shock, a feeling I hadn't had since opening the vial itself.

"I thought you didn't notice," I said, pushing him backward so that I could see the look in his eyes.

"It is completely extraordinary. How could I not?"

"You told me that you didn't understand what all the excitement was about."

"Would you be here otherwise?"

"Is it the only reason you want to paint me?"

I sounded pathetic even to myself.

"It's the only reason. It's not your face or your hair or your limbs," he said, staring at my body. "Those are things that every woman has and some women have them much more beautifully than you."

"Please, don't insult me. Not now."

"I'm telling you the truth. If the truth hurts you, so be it."

Michael took the inside of my arm and slid it across his face.

"But your beautiful, exotic, erotic, sweet, sweet skin. No one in this whole wide world has what you do."

He crouched in front of me at eye level, holding on to my hair. Much as I wanted to prove that I was more than just the content of the vial left to me by my grandmother, it was already too late for me to hate him, and against my will my whole body wanted to touch him. It was as if hundreds of tiny glass vials of liquid desire were breaking inside of me, but I sat perfectly still and did not reach out.

He dropped my hair and walked back over to his canvas.

"I've wanted to capture your scent in my work since the moment I met you. Its silent, unobtrusive beauty and spectacular uniqueness is exactly what is missing from my painting. If I could somehow get it inside of a canvas I know that the results would be unparalleled."

He turned the air-conditioning off and the heat on.

"It will make your scent more distinct and powerful," he said, "just like it was at the Broken Heart Ballroom, and my hands will stay warmer too."

The studio was unbearably hot as Michael worked. My skin and clothes were wet with sweat and I could smell the rise of the jasmine first and then the red velvet rose, the fire, and finally the strong scent of leather. He put his brush down and came over to the pew and put his face as close to mine as he could without making contact.

"So hard to stay away from you," he said in a breathy half sentence. "I'm afraid of you, Evangeline. Afraid that you won't come back. You'll get scared. You'll leave this place and look at Gabriel and you won't come home to me."

"This isn't my home. And please don't say his name out loud."

But it didn't matter whether or not he said Gabriel's name, because he was right. I already knew I wouldn't come back, I couldn't. He was a danger to my life with Gabriel. A threat to our happiness.

"I'm here now and I'm not leaving," I said. "Finish the painting as best you can. Paint all night if you have to. Paint like you're never going to see me again."

Michael went back to the canvas but I could tell that he had lost some of his original fire.

He put down his brush.

"It's not working," he said. "To be honest, it hasn't been working since we started. I need something from you, Evangeline. Something I can mix into the paint. A lock of hair, a fingernail, or a small piece of skin."

I looked at my manicured nails and the long strands of my hair and knew I would not part with either of them for Michael and his painting.

I walked through the house and let myself out, leaving Michael in his studio imagining my nakedness and dreaming of body parts to mix into his paints.

43

Sitting alone in the garden back at the apartment on St. Louis, which was really Michael's apartment, I knew that the strangeness of the white room, finding Gabriel in Louise's kitchen, opening the ruby glass vial, and the threat of Rayanne Crabbe were nothing compared with the pull of Michael Bon Chance and New Orleans.

I was tired from the day and I lay down in bed. I did not want to become greedy with her words but I was hoping that Louise would have a message for me, a direction inside a dream that was worth taking in this directionless time.

I held the empty red vial against my chest, absorbing every last bit of her—and then I fell asleep and dreamed a riddle of her making.

Too still I am in death
Too fast I am in trouble
Too cold I'll cause you fear

Too hot it will be double.
Life I can be, on the inside
Death I can be, on the outside.
The problem cannot be solved in your mind
Nor in your soul
But in the very depth
Of your very bones.

When I woke up I wrote down the words with a perfection of memory that surprised me, but no matter how many times I read them, I could not make any sense of them at all. I was more confused than before. She was telling me to use my instinct and to follow what I felt in my bones. Didn't she know that my instincts were not to be trusted at best and at their very worst, were completely nonexistent?

I waited until the sun went down to walk along Royal Street. I had become more and more attracted to Madame Susteen, whose prophecy that I would bring misery and destruction to those I loved seemed to become truer with each passing day in New Orleans. I stole a look into her parlor-floor shop, same as I did every time I walked by, but this time was different. This time Michael was inside.

He stood at the counter talking to Madame Susteen. There were jars and bottles and potions between them on the glass countertop. I watched as he opened his wallet and placed several bills in front of her. I remembered that she had a dislike of taking money directly from the hands of a customer and he seemed to know that fact as well. After he put the bills down, she handed him a small glass decanter. I turned my eyes away. I'd been in New Orleans long enough to know that if I stayed even one moment longer she would know for sure that I was at the door, and I could not risk another encounter.

Gabriel came home late that night. So late that I was already in bed trying to sleep. I listened to the movements of his life as if I were spying on him. I heard him opening and closing the refrigerator, scraping a pan across the burner on the stove, pouring liquid into a glass. It all sounded as close as a whisper. As if I had developed some kind of extrasensory hearing.

He came into the bedroom, sat on the end of the bed, and took off his shoes, pants, and shirt. He went into the bathroom. I could hear the toothbrush scraping against his teeth and I swear I was able to differentiate between the front teeth, the incisors, and the molars in the back.

He got underneath the covers and put his arms around me. He was naked and ready. I let him touch my body, pretending to be asleep. I liked it that way sometimes, when I could relax, and imagine, and not have to move or do anything physical at all.

I lay there and focused on his hands but all my mind could think of was Michael in Madame Susteen's parlor. *What was he doing there?* I wondered as Gabriel touched my breasts. She had told me that she could create a scent that would bind Gabriel to me if I wanted such a thing to happen. Maybe Michael had purchased a scent that would bind me to *him*. That would coax me to remove my clothes and then cut off my hair and fingernails to mix in with his paints.

I tried as hard as I could to switch my focus to Gabriel, but Michael and Madame Susteen were implanted in my thoughts and working against our happiness.

I drifted off to sleep and woke up to Gabriel's hands between my legs, but my mind, like a rebellious child, was still on Michael. I could feel his mouth on places it had never been and his hands in my hair where they had.

I pulled Gabriel closer. He lay on top of me and wrapped his arms around my back. He held me tight like he knew I liked, but the presence of Michael was too strong, and against my will it was he and I who were together. I could see the water nymphs on the wall of the studio, feel the smooth wood of the church pews, smell his skin, and feel his cool, cool hands on my body.

After Gabriel had fallen asleep I couldn't get the idea out of my head that Madame Susteen's potion, whatever liquid was inside the glass decanter Michael had purchased, had made it possible for him to reach me telepathically. And what he was communicating was pure desire.

I closed my eyes and accepted the fact that the only thing keeping me from going straight to the lilac Victorian that very moment was the weight of Gabriel's body on mine.

44

Levon brought me another cupcake for breakfast, chocolate frosting with yellow cake underneath. I set it down on the kitchen table and stared at it, its bright, multicolored sprinkles mocking the way I felt.

"You look tired," he said.

"I'm just thinking."

"About what?"

"Life."

"When I'm confused, I take my mama's cards. I pick one and I let it tell me what to do."

"Tarot cards?" I asked out loud, wondering silently whether reading them was a prerequisite to living in New Orleans.

"Of course. You really don't know a lot, do you?"

"No, I really don't."

"I'll be right back. Leave the door open. I'm gonna get the deck."

"I'm sure there's one in this house somewhere," I said.

"No. My mama's always works best for me. She says I was born with a tarot deck under my butt."

It was hard to believe it had come to this: a fourteen-year-old boy was going to tell me what to do with my life based on a deck of cards. But the way things were going it seemed just as likely as anything else to be the right course of action.

"Okay," said Levon, slightly out of breath from running between his apartment and mine, "I'm gonna shuffle the cards and lay them out on the table facedown. You're gonna pick one and I'm gonna tell you what it means. Got it?"

"How often do you do this?"

"When I can't decide what to do in a serious situation."

"You're fourteen. How many serious situations do you find yourself in?"

"Not too many, but the ones I have to figure out are important. Like if I should go visit my old grandma in Bayou Jolie, or if a cupcake should be chocolate or red velvet or orange cake. A decision like that could change your whole day. Make you feel one way or another one, depending on your choice."

Levon spread the cards on the table. The deck had a solid black backing and I had a negative feeling about the cards.

"Okay, pick one," he said. "Take your time, but don't take too much, I got things to do. And whatever you do, don't look at the card. Just hand it over to me."

"You're kind of bossy, you know that?"

"It's a flaw. I'm working on it."

I looked over the spread. I thought about what it would mean to pick from the left, the right, or the center. I chose the very last card on the left.

"Wow. I have to say, Evangeline, in all my years I've never seen anyone pick that card. Most folks go for the center. The far left makes you an anomaly."

"Big word," I said, and he smiled his most winning smile.

Levon placed the card faceup on the table. The Magician. He turned it over and over in his hands.

"Well?"

"I'm thinking about how to phrase myself," he said.

I didn't want to tell him that I was all too familiar with the Magician.

"There's someone in your life," he said. "Someone you know who can talk you into anything. His words are like magic. For good or for bad."

"How do I know which?"

"You don't. Until you do."

"Well, that's not helpful."

"It is what it is."

"Should I see this person again?"

"If you want magic words for good or for bad."

"Would you?"

"Sure. Magic words are better than plain old words any day."

"Even if they're for bad?"

"There's all kind of bad. Some bad is even good."

"How old are you?"

"If it works out well for you I can help you arrange your day, every day, if you want me to. My old grandma says I have the gift."

"Let's see how this one goes," I said.

"See ya later."

"Levon?"

"Yeah?"

"Does the black color of the cards bother you?"

"Nah. I got more pressing things on my mind. Besides, it's just darkness, like when you sleep and dream. It's a good thing if you look at it that way."

"I guess."

"Here, take the card with you," he said. "But remember to give it back to me and whatever you do, don't lose it."

"I thought this was your lucky deck?"

"I said don't lose it, didn't I?"

I was pretty sure that Levon gave me the card because he was feeling lonely and he wanted to be certain that he would see me again soon, so I took it and made sure he watched as I put it in the back pocket of my jeans.

45

The waitress at Johnny River's didn't treat me any better this time than last.

"You want coffee?" she asked.

"Yes, please."

She brought it over, once again without any sugar or cream. I didn't say anything this time. Not that I was afraid of her, or proud, I was just too busy staring at the Victorian across the street. Michael and his magic words were either inside waiting for me, or at Madame Susteen's, creating elixirs with the intent of wrecking my future with Gabriel.

I realized those were the only two places my mind could imagine him. I knew nothing about his life.

"You want something to eat? Eggs?"

"Eggs?"

"Yeah, those round white things that drop from chickens."

"They're oval."

"You want them or not?"

"Okay. Two, scrambled."

A few minutes later she came back with the eggs, a new napkin, and a glass of water. She set them down and came back with salt and pepper. It was as though we had come to some kind of sudden truce that had arisen from nowhere.

"Hey, Eggs!"

I was already across the street when I turned around to see the waitress yelling for me through the screen door of the diner.

"Eggs! You forgot something."

The face of the Magician was pressed against the screen. I had dropped Levon's card.

"You always carry a black tarot card with you to breakfast?" she asked.

"This is the first time."

"I bet. I gotta ask you though, why the Magician?"

"A friend gave it to me. Why? What do you know about it?"

"I know you got yourself involved with a black-back magician. That means everything is hidden, and backward. You could run into an animal that doesn't act like one. A magical animal like a rougarou. A werewolf that feasts on evil souls."

I put the card in my back pocket, horizontally so it wouldn't fall out this time.

"Protect your soul, Eggs."

"I'm not evil," I said, already out the door and on the way to see Michael, who seemed more normal to me at that moment than the waitress at Johnny River's.

"We're all capable of it sometimes," she yelled behind me.

46

I followed Michael into the room with the fountain. It was running and water dripped slowly over the stone cherubs. A century from now they'll be nothing more than pebbles, I thought. That's what dripping water does. So cooly innocent until it grinds you down and washes you away without a trace.

"You know, I did a portrait of Johnny River when he was still alive," said Michael. "It was just about the time he was opening up the diner. He was a very good-looking man in his day. He wore seersucker suits, a straw hat, and white shoes. That was Johnny River."

"I'm not here to sit for you today," I said. "I'm here to ask you a question."

I knew I had to ask quickly, as the sound of the fountain was making me lose my nerve.

"I saw you yesterday, in Madame Susteen's parlor."

"Ah," said Michael. "And you're wondering what I was doing in there?"

"I am."

"I've lived in this town a long time, Evangeline, and I've known Susteen for years. I did a portrait of her once, way back. She bought it and then she burned it to the ground. She said it was dangerous to have a likeness of herself hanging around the house. On the day you saw us, she was mixing something special for me like she does for half the people in this town. Is there a problem with that?"

"I think she has evil intentions," I said.

"She has her ways, I know, but I'm going to be painting you, so why would I want to cause you harm? And why would she? What could possibly result from that?"

I didn't know how to tell him that I could feel him inside of my body when I was in bed with Gabriel and I thought it had to do with Madame Susteen and her potions. I didn't know how to tell myself that I could feel him inside of my body and it might have to do with my own desire.

Michael crossed the room to the fireplace and took a small crystal decanter from the mantelpiece.

"If it will make you feel better, this is what she made for me."

He brought the crystal toward me. The scent coming out of the cut glass was heady—nothing compared to my own, of course, but still I could smell it before it was anywhere close to my face.

"It is true that I was there because of you," he said, "but it's not what you think. I was there in case you didn't come back to me. It was a distinct possibility, I knew, so I asked her to replicate your scent as best she could."

"How did she know what it was?"

"I went to see her right after you left my house. I didn't wash my hands after running them through your hair. She took your scent from my fingertips."

The thought of Madame Susteen sniffing Michael's hands made me queasy.

"I asked her to do it once, to smell my skin, and she wouldn't even consider it," I said. "She wouldn't take the scent from my body into hers. She said she was too old to take the chance."

"So?"

"So why would she do it for you and not me?"

"She doesn't like you," said Michael, "she told me that herself. She said it wasn't a personal feeling; it originated in the cards."

"Yes, I remember. She told me I would bring death and destruction to the people who loved me."

"She didn't mention that," said Michael, taking several steps away from me. "She did say that the blue lotus, which is very rare, is most closely aligned as far as she could tell with your skin. It's what she gave me, in the decanter. She doesn't understand your scent. It's a mystery to her and that's why she's so afraid of you."

I could not remember Louise ever mentioning blue lotus.

"She can't decipher you, not even with the help of the cards. You're already way past her. It won't be Susteen who can give you the answers you're looking for, that's for sure. It will be someone stronger than her. Someone who's not afraid."

"Do you think she was right? That I'll kill the people closest to me?"

"Maybe. In one way or another. 'Kill' is a subjective word. It's not always physical."

I thought about what Michael had done to the psychiatrist he was dating.

"Are you afraid I'm going to be the end of you?" I asked.

His smile was boyish and engaging, as if even his demise, should it come to that, would be charming.

"The end of me might be a good thing. Maybe I'll become something else. Something better. Anyway, being afraid of a human being is nothing. We're here for such a short period of time, so what does it matter, scared, not scared; what matters is that we last. That's why the blue lotus is so important."

"Why?"

"In legends, immortals are attracted to its scent. Vampires, werewolves, that sort of thing. That's why the ancient Egyptians called it the scent of immortality."

I took Levon's card out of my pocket and rotated the Magician between my fingers. Magical words for good or bad.

"Gabriel told me that you painted werewolves."

"I have painted the odd rougarou from time to time."

"But you don't believe in them?"

"I believe in immortality in whatever form it takes. Paintings, books, music, werewolves. They're all the same—the desire to last forever. In my opinion, every artist is a vampire or a werewolf, or a thief. All we want is to live on and on through the work we do and we'll take whatever we can from the people unlucky enough to be around us—their stories, pieces of their selves, their very souls if they'll let us, which they so often do with surprising ease—in order to reach our creative goals. How is that different from a vampire?"

"Can I see the paintings?"

Michael went over to the far side of the studio to a stack of canvases. He chose ten paintings and lined them up along the wall. I bent down to look at them. They were charcoal drawings of tiny wolves, small, deadly things made even more sinister against the backdrop of the beautiful sea nymphs.

He came and stood behind me. He put both of his palms against the wall, one on either side of me.

"They're good. They're very good," I said, aware that with one step backward my head would be against his chest, one step closer and it would be near the tiny mouths of the waiting wolves.

"Good enough to make you want to sit for me?" he whispered into my hair, his words vibrating into the base of my skull.

I closed my eyes and held on to my innocence for the remaining seconds of its life. It wasn't the paintings that made me want to sit for Michael. It was the closeness of his body, his smooth, hairless chest under the antique smoking jacket, and the feel of his breath in my hair. It was the ropes and veins of his arms pressing the wall on either side of me and the memory of his body in my bed the night before, even though we were not in the same room, the same house, or even in the same part of town.

"Yes," I said in a distant, faraway voice that I hardly recognized as my own, "I want to sit for you."

"Will you give me what I need?"

"What do you need?"

"Everything. But we can start small."

47

Michael took my hand and we walked through the lilac Victorian. We didn't go into the studio but into the bedroom and then the bathroom. The fixtures were gold and the floor was black marble and there was a crystal chandelier on the ceiling. I'd never seen such a thing in a bathroom before. The tub was old, deep, and ornate; the water ran out of the open mouth of an antique gilded dolphin.

"It's from Greece," he said, turning on the faucet and watching the steaming water rush out of the mammal. "The hot water will make you that much more fragrant."

Michael filled the tub with soapy water and left the room. I didn't take off my clothes. I wore my skin-colored body suit like a bathing suit and sank into the bath. The water was burning hot and I accepted it as punishment for whatever it was that I was about to do.

Michael came back into the room. He stood over me, breathing in the vapors coming from the tub, drawing them toward him with his hands, using his palms to wash the mist over his head, as if that alone might make him a better painter.

"The heat," I said, "it's unbearable."

"Sssssshhhhh," he said. "You'll get used to it."

He opened the mirrored medicine cabinet and took out a shaving kit with a silver-handled razor and brush.

"It's made from human hair. The softest there is. I bought it especially for you. Only the best for my Evangeline."

I did not bother to correct him. To say that I was Gabriel's Evangeline, or Evangeline's Evangeline, because in that moment I was not completely sure whose Evangeline I truly was.

"It will grow back," he said. "It's no loss to you and it means everything to me."

He lathered up the brush with a scentless soap. He handed me the razor and sat on the bathroom floor next to the tub. I draped one leg over the side, thankful for the coolness of the ceramic tile, and began shaving my leg. Michael held out his hand and after each stroke I wiped the tiny hairs caught in the blade across his palm, careful not to cut the skin. I hadn't finished my calf when he asked me if he could try.

"Let me," he said.

I nodded and fixed my gaze on the water, watching yet another little piece of my innocence float away on a bubble of soap.

He took the razor and carefully, so much more carefully than I ever could have done myself, he shaved my legs. He started at the ankle, and holding my foot in his hand he made clean, smooth strokes around the delicate bone. He worked his way over my calves and knees and up to my thighs without missing a single hair while I laid my head back on a pillow that hung over the edge of the bath and stared at the chandelier on the ceiling, pretending.

When he was done I swirled my fingertip through the tiny hairs in his hand.

"What are you going to do with these?"

"I'm going to mix them into my paints."

He drew the wet hairs together with his fingertips and wiped them into an empty silver bowl on the floor next to him and then he brought his palm up to his nose. He inhaled deeply and then held his hand up to my face and it was true, the hair had left behind the scents of jasmine, red velvet rose, fire, and the deep, natural, and earthy tang of leather.

"If I can infuse your scent into my paintings then people will be drawn to them just like they're drawn to you, without ever knowing why, and without ever suspecting. The only thing they'll know for sure is that they have to have the canvas, and they will be willing to pay a high price for it. They'll place it front and center in their sitting rooms and all their friends will want to purchase one too. Just imagine, a Michael Bon Chance in every home in New Orleans."

He spoke with a mania in his voice, on and on with no breaks and no clear punctuation in his thoughts.

"Don't you think they would want them anyway, without the scent?" I asked, breaking into his run-on sentence when I had the chance. "Don't you have any belief in yourself as an artist?"

"I know the level of my skill, Evangeline. I'm too old to kid myself about things like that."

"What about the mermaids on the wall? Those are good."

"I copied them from other people's work. Famous people. I could never come up with those ideas on my own. You are my key, Evangeline, my one chance, and together we will be fantastically wealthy and famous. I know we will."

He held on to my legs while he spoke, wrapping his arms around them as if they were a part of his own body, and when he had finished talking he put them back in the bath, shaved my arms from the fingertips to the shoulders and then, raising them up, he brought the blade down under each one, making sure to collect all of the thousands of tiny fibers in the bowl on the bathroom floor.

"Why are you letting me do this?" he asked.

"Because I'm getting tired."

"Of?"

"Of being so desired by other people. Of being beholden to this gift, as if I somehow have to live up to it. I have to be good and beautiful and perfect to deserve it. And I'm none of those things. I'm sick of people responding to my scent as if it's truly who I am."

"You feel guilty for having something so beautiful."

"You can take it all. I want to give it away."

"It's why you have no drive, you know. No real ambition. No desire to go to school or get a job. You were given something so extraordinary that you don't need any of those things. It's like being born beautiful, except beauty fades, and this may very well stay with you forever."

He was right. The scent was not only making it impossible for me to go outside, but it was weakening me. Making me direction-less. Way back, long before I knew Michael or even Gabriel, I used to be plain to look at. Not bad, but not exceptionally beautiful in any way. Not repellent, but not attracting. Not the first picked, not the last. But that was *me,* and in the months since I'd opened the vial I had all but forgotten who I was.

つ

Michael asked me to take off the bodysuit and shave the parts that he was not allowed to touch. And when he left the bathroom and closed the door behind him, I did. When I was finished I stood looking at my body in the long oval mirror. Steam rose from my strange hairless shape and fogged up the glass until I was not there at all. I stared at the emptiness, losing myself in the glass until I saw another shape in the mirror. Faint at first, but there they were, Michael's dark eyes, staring at my naked body through the half-opened bathroom door. I focused on the mirror, hoping to disappear in the vapors.

"What are you looking for?" Michael whispered from the other side of the door.

"Yesterday," I said to myself. "I'm looking for yesterday."

⌇

I wrapped my body in a towel and Michael came back into the bathroom to wash the razor in the sink. Neither of us mentioned the trespassing he had done with his eyes.

"The hair will grow back," he said.

"And you'll shave it off again, and again, as many times as you need."

He seemed pleased.

"May I?" he asked, picking up a hairbrush.

"Yes."

He brushed the hair on my head until it hung perfectly straight down my back.

"I want some of this too," he whispered, the covetousness apparent in his voice.

"That's Gabriel's favorite part of me," I said.

I felt as if I were talking to Michael in a dream.

"Just a little trim. The fragrance is very special here."

He lifted my hair to look at the back of my neck. Then he took a small pair of silver nail scissors and trimmed a quarter of an inch of my hair. I didn't say a word. He collected the strands and put them into the bowl with the rest. I had a sudden desire to shave it all off, to get rid of every single hair on my head, but I didn't tell him that for fear that in the quickness of a single breath, his greed would take it all. And my desire would let him.

"Tell me again why you let me," he said.

"Because I know what you want, and I know I can give it to you, and everything is clear as day and I'm useful. With Gabriel, I don't know what he wants. He doesn't seem to want anything from me at all."

Michael ran his fingers through the wet hair in the bowl. The little ones from my legs stuck to his hands and got under his nails.

"It's like your soul is on the outside of your body, and now I've got some of it for myself."

He turned his back toward me.

"The gallery owners and collectors say my paintings lack feeling. They say that I'm technically talented, that I can paint and draw with the best of them, but that my work has no emotion."

"That's a terrible thing to say. How do they know?"

"They know."

"Even if they're right, I doubt my body hair can give your paintings a soul."

"I'm not so sure. Scent is something that people don't understand. Its very nothingness can change people's moods, feelings, days and nights, even their sexuality at the core of their beings. Let's just say I'm doing a sort of experiment. Right now I'm an alchemist who will try to change something base, like my paintings, into something extraordinary and desirable."

I was silenced by how much Michael sounded like Louise when he talked about scent. For one split second, I thought that maybe he was an evil reincarnation of her. Her negative side, come to life. It gave me chills to think that negative Louise had stolen a look at my naked body and shaved my legs and arms in the bathtub.

48

I walked as fast as I could along Magazine Street. Past the antique furniture stores, vintage clothing stores, the rare-book store and the hard-to-find record store in the back of the diner, with the early Cajun recordings from the thirties. I wondered whether anything in this town was new. At that moment the city of New Orleans felt oppressive, old, hot, and very small and tight, like an animal's travel cage.

Gabriel was already home when I walked through the door— the one time I needed to be alone he was right there. He'd left the library early as if he'd had some special radar tuned toward my attraction to another man, and was sitting at the kitchen table, waiting for me to arrive. We shared a cup of coffee but he was impatient and he drew me to him. I knew it was my scent, so strong from the overheated studio and the steaming hot bath. I didn't even have time to finish my coffee before his hands were on my legs, under my skirt, where Michael's had been less than an hour before.

He was hungry for me, as greedy as Michael was for my skin and hair. He took off my clothes right there in the kitchen and kissed me hard with my back against the refrigerator door. He ran his hands over the new smoothness of my body without suspicion. We lay down on the tile floor, which anywhere else in the world would have been cold except for New Orleans, where nothing ever was.

I closed my eyes, wanting to erase the day and be happy with my love, Gabriel, but all I could see was Michael. I could hear his voice whispering in my ear, *I need more. I want to be loved like you, Evangeline.* It was *his* chest I saw coming down on me. His icy hands making me press my hips into Gabriel. I knew it then, lying there on the floor, that there was no escaping him. He would have me anyway, without my consent, through his access to my mind. Lying on the kitchen floor I wanted him so much I came close to calling his name. I opened my eyes and looked at Gabriel and all I saw was loss.

I thought about the Broken Heart Ballroom and how I'd already known that he was gone. I held his body tight to mine. I thought that if I let go I would somehow find myself back at the lilac Victorian. I knew then that not only was I failing myself but I was failing Louise too. She never would have wanted things to turn out this way. This could not have been part of her plan when she left the vial for me. She would never want me to hurt the one I loved so much.

"You're so beautiful now," Gabriel whispered in my ear. "Ever since we came to New Orleans."

I wondered how he could mistake the growing desire I had for another man for beauty.

"You have a mysteriousness that you didn't have when I met you, not even after we opened the vial," he whispered.

"It's just the heat," I said "that's all," and then I pressed his head to my neck so that he could not look into my eyes and find the truth.

⸎

Later that night, in bed, we made love again. Cats screamed from the courtyard below, the spooky, pornographic, wailing cry of felines in heat. I don't know why but it embarrassed me to be with Gabriel while the tomcats and queens were doing the same thing as the two of us.

"Do you think they can smell you?" he asked.

"I hope not."

"Are the windows closed?"

"They are."

If I thought I could not possibly feel worse, I was wrong.

The cats cried for hours. The monotone droning irritated my nerves. How could they want each other enough to scream for it all night long? And then my mind drifted to Michael, who I could feel silently screaming for me through the windows of the house on Magazine Street.

"Are you asleep?" asked Gabriel.

I didn't answer.

I remembered reading that if you have a cat in heat you have to lock it up and make sure it can't escape otherwise it will be gone for days, returning only after it has mated and conceived. I hoped

Gabriel had read the same thing. I hoped that he would lock me up and hide the key.

The cats outside were telling me what I couldn't tell myself. *Stay inside,* they said in their eerie growl, *stay inside.* I'd always had a great affinity for cats. I believed in them, in their intelligence and their sheer beauty, and I considered them enviable creatures to be reckoned with.

49

Gabriel never did follow the advice of the felines, and without any locks on the doors of my mind I went back to see Michael. On the one hand I was interested to see if the idea could work, on the other I wanted to find out whether I could diminish, or even lose, the power of the scent in my body by giving it to him, and on the third, invisible but weighty hand, I had no will at all to stop what was happening between us.

In the weeks that followed, lacking anything resembling control, I gave Michael everything I could. When I was around him I wanted to give away as much as possible in order to free myself of the incredible burden the scent had become. And of course he took it all without hesitation. Not just the leg shavings, which he scooped out of the bathwater as they floated on top or clung to the sides of the tub when the water was gone, but every long strand that wrapped itself around the bristles of my brush, carefully unraveling each one as if it were made of gold. A scab on my elbow worked, fingernail clippings, toenails, the liquid from absolutely anything that came in contact with my mouth—forks, spoons, or toothbrush. He gathered up the things I used as though they were gemstones. He hoarded them, and then mixed them in his ceramic bowls.

As time passed he got what he wanted and his paints began to smell more and more like me. I could still detect the strong, oily paint fumes, but the jasmine, rose, fire, and leather of my body were predominant.

He painted all sorts of things; it made no difference to him, as it was not an exact image he was after, and all he cared about was the scent of the paint. He made flowers and demons, stars, suns, and ragged children with broken bodies. Ideas and images filtered ceaselessly out of his imagination, unchecked. He did not even bother to paint me. My portrait was largely forgotten. He used my body for what it could give him, for its scent only, until the day that he didn't.

I remember. I lay on my back on the church pew in my skin-colored bodysuit while Michael took a vinyl record out of its sleeve and put a Cajun ballad on the record player. Unaccompanied, a woman's voice sang a haunting, plaintive song of loss. Of losing her land, her home, and the man she loved. I stared at the blue water on the ceiling above me and felt as though at any moment it was going to come pouring down on top of me, like a monsoon or a hurricane. And then, finally, he began to work on my portrait.

The first scratch of the bristles across the canvas sounded like a wave crashing on the shore. I closed my eyes and dreamed of Louise. The sound of the brush going back and forth seemed to erase the layers of my brain and I remembered little things about her, like the way she always wore a brooch. A "piece," she called it. She had a drawer full of them and she would put one on before going out to see her friends. Her outfit was never complete without it. "Just remember not to stick yourself when you put it on," she'd say. "You don't want to become your own voodoo doll."

"Evangeline," said Michael. His voice so close it seemed to come from inside my own head.

I opened my eyes and looked at him.

"I'm sorry. I was thinking," I said, "or dreaming."

I had no idea which one.

He sat down next to me.

"There is one more thing I need from you."

And there it was again, the pull that came from the sound of his voice. The spell he wrapped around me whenever he was close. He was a sorcerer, even if he did not believe it. Even if he was never able to change his paintings into works of art, he had changed me from not wanting him to wanting him just by his nearness.

From my position on the pew he looked upside down—just like the magician on the tarot card. And like Rosemary, Levon, and the waitress at Johnny River's had said—everything would be turned around.

"What do you want?" I asked him. "What is it?"

He leaned his face over mine until his mouth was hovering just over my lips.

"This," he whispered.

I could feel the air from his lungs drift into mine. And then it was me who lifted my head ever so slightly and opened my mouth on his.

The kiss came as a shock, although it shouldn't have. By the time his face was this close to mine, it was so long in coming, it was already perfected. Had already been done a thousand times by each of us, separately, alone.

It was like the first time I'd been with Gabriel, except that I'd wanted to do that—I was a willing participant. This was something different. It's not that I was being forced, I wasn't, I was simply experiencing a loss of will. A strange, uncontrollable pull that was definitely not love but also was.

Michael slid his hands over my shoulders and down to my waist. His tenderness alarmed me.

"Let's go, Evangeline," he said.

He stood up, took both of my hands in his, and pulled me from the pew. He started walking us backward out of the studio and in the direction of his bedroom, but I could not follow. Maybe I was frightened. Maybe somewhere in my mind I did not want it to begin. Somewhere I knew that I could never stop it and never survive it. He took my hand and pulled it toward himself roughly. And right then I felt that I had to get away from him, that I was too close to him. I could already feel the loss of Gabriel, even though nothing more than a single kiss had transpired.

And so we did not go into the bedroom. Instead, he unbuttoned the buttons of his shirt and I pressed my face against his chest. With his skin crushed under my cheek I could feel my tears for Gabriel sliding over Michael's heartbeat.

"I can't give you any more." I pushed him away. "I won't make love to you. Ever. It would be impossible."

I hoped he understood that I wanted him to take my scent, but not my love for Gabriel along with it.

I felt his ice-cold hand on my shoulder and then my will began to weaken once again. I started to cry. I hadn't cried in a long time, not since Louise died, and all the stored-up tears dripped down my face and onto my neck. I was soaking wet with tears. I'd heard that expression before and disliked it because it sounded impossible, but just then I knew that it wasn't.

Michael pulled a waiting tissue out of his pocket as if he knew beforehand that his suggestion would make me cry. He pressed it against my face and my neck. He sopped up the tears and then raced over to his ceramic bowl to mix them in with his paint.

"You don't care about anything else," I said in a voice that had the emotion of a yell but the choke of a whisper.

"Susteen told me," he said with a chill in his voice, "that part of your scent comes from the brine of tears. She said I needed to make you cry. I knew that with my hands on you, you would think of your precious Gabriel and feel the beginning of the loss."

I backed away.

"Evangeline," Michael said in a voice that sounded like begging, "I want to be loved as much as you are. I sit here day after day and wonder, why you? Why were you given this gift and not me? Sometimes I think that God loves you more than other people. I know he loves you more than me."

I ran from the studio and stumbled out of the house. I lost my way along Magazine Street, a street I had walked every day for what felt like my entire life. Finally, I found the courthouse, the landmark I used to find my way home in the Quarter in the dark. Even though in that moment I knew there were no more landmarks and no more ways home.

I sat down on the stone steps and fell asleep with my head on my lap. A man came up to me. "Miss," he said, "are you okay?"

I do not remember answering him. I do not remember getting up from the steps and walking through the midnight danger of New Orleans to Gabriel's and my apartment on St. Louis.

I do remember sitting down on the wide-planked floor underneath the chandelier in my nude bodysuit, green skirt, and sandals. I did not turn on the lights. I did not get into my bed. I listened to the electric brush of the street cleaners and watched the streetlight like moonlight through the blinds.

I sat with my back against the wall, thinking. I knew there were no ifs. No point in wondering if we were going to have an affair. If it would be good. Or if I even wanted to go ahead with it. I was simply thinking of how it would be.

50

The day came when Michael was finally ready to show his work. I had not seen him since our kiss, but he called the apartment on St. Louis constantly, begging me to help him greet the gallery owner, insistent and demanding as a baby when it came to my presence, and I gave in to him as I had always done.

We stood in front of the trickling fountain in the sitting room and greeted the woman as she came through the door. We walked her through the house and back into the studio, flanking her on either side as if we had both made the paintings, which, in a sense, we had.

She spent a long time with each image, the stars and flowers, and the portraits of the women in the park. But it was the one single painting of me, the one with my hair over my breasts like the water nymph, that she liked best. It was not a nude, as my breasts were covered and my legs crossed, but the church pew was a perfect foil and somehow it made me look even more naked than an actual nude.

"Lovely, just lovely," she said.

In truth I did not know whether to be happy or sad. I turned to look at Michael, who was of course beyond elated, showing not the slightest bit of concern or confusion. If it had been my work I would have wondered whether I had any real talent. I would have been upset that I could not sell it without the liquid insides of the woman standing next to me. But Michael was only interested in the gallery owner's love of the work and the potential for fame that it held.

"These are very, very good," she said. "I'm not making any promises, but I believe I could do wonders for you, and I would like to build a show around your work. Of course, I'll have to bring in my colleagues to take a look, but really, I don't see anyone having a problem with any of them at all. I believe you've done it, Mr. Bon Chance. You're going to have a solo show."

Michael looked like he was in a daze, and I have to admit that no matter how I felt about Michael and me and all that had transpired, it was fascinating to watch someone's dream come true right in front of my eyes.

A few days later, as expected, the owner's colleagues agreed with her assessment, and Michael was offered a show at their prestigious gallery on Royal Street. The painter from the neighborhood who everyone knew from his years of portraiture in the park was about to make it big.

I never once believed that Michael got the show because of me. In truth I thought it was his powerful, almost unshakable new confidence in his work that generated the interest. That plus the sheer amount of painting he had done in a short period of time fueled by his conviction that my scent would make him famous. It was

those intangibles that Michael could never understand, that made
his work suddenly more palatable to the dealers and collectors who
ruled the art world.

کچ

In an effort to make sure the scent of the paint didn't fade before
the show, a catastrophe he would do anything to avoid, Michael
added the blue lotus, the scent of immortality he'd purchased from
Madame Susteen, in the hope that it would add longevity to the
paint. Sometimes he used only the blue lotus without any addition
from my body, but those works were never as good, and ultimately
they generated only minimal interest. Still, I believed that he did
not have as much faith in those pieces he worked on without me
and that's what caused them to remain unsold. He had put a psy-
chological hex on the work that he did by himself without the help
of my body.

51

The gallery opening was crowded. The line wrapped around Royal
Street and then some. It seemed that all of New Orleans had turned
out to see Michael's work. The temperature hovered around ninety
degrees, which he said was good news as far as the scent coming
off the paintings and into the crowd filled with wealthy people with
open wallets.

When Gabriel arrived he looked sharp. He had on a light summer suit and a white shirt. His black hair shone like a dark, glassy
lake, rippling over the blue collar of his jacket.

We were walking toward the long line of people when Michael
came over and put a cold arm around Gabriel.

"It's been a long while, my friend and tenant."

"Yes it has," said Gabriel. "Too long."

"And now it's time for you to come inside and take a look at what we've done."

"We?"

"Evangeline and I. Hasn't she told you about the paintings?"

"Not much."

"He's busy with school," I said.

"Well, I think you're going to love them," said Michael. "Really I do. I'm excited for you to see them."

He winked in my direction and the slow closing of his eyelid startled me.

"Evangeline," he said, "I think you are going to be very surprised as well."

"Why?" I asked. "Why would I be surprised?"

"You'll see," he said. "I painted them from my imagination, just as you suggested." He leaned over and whispered in my ear, "I hope they make you proud."

I had a bad feeling and I dragged myself toward the door as if I were moving toward an execution, with slow feet and a racing mind.

⌇

What was inside the gallery stunned me perhaps even more than Gabriel. Gone were the flowers and demons. Nowhere in sight were the suns and the stars and the ragged children with broken bodies. Instead, there were three large rooms, twelve walls in all, and each one was covered with images of my nude body in all modes of expression.

Legs wide open, mouth smiling in pleasure, smoking cigarettes, drinking whiskey, laughing, crying, stripping off clothing, lying down, and taking a bath in that black marble bathroom with the crystal chandelier and the gold dolphin faucet.

Ghostly pale nudes on bloodred backgrounds, all there for

Gabriel to see with his very own innocent eyes. The canvases were large, and the genitals crystal clear. It was as if I had invited Gabriel into a torture chamber built just for him.

There was no way I could have prepared him for what he saw, and Michael knew it. I had been so preoccupied with Michael himself that I'd neglected to consider what he was capable of and to what lengths he would go to have me for himself, to secure his muse and his key to the art world, and, especially, to rid himself of Gabriel, the man who stood in the way of his dream.

I tried to imagine my own response had Gabriel been alone with an artist for several weeks. I tried to picture myself viewing the finished work, coming to the realization that Gabriel had never had his clothes on in the presence of this woman, not even in the beginning when they had just met. I'm sure it would have been my undoing. A complete destruction.

I could feel Gabriel's terrible sadness and I could not bear that he felt that way. Standing on the threshold of the gallery I hoped I would be able to convince him that only a single kiss had passed between Michael and me. I caught myself holding my breath as we went farther inside. Maybe if I held it long enough I could permanently avoid the fallout.

Gabriel and I stood next to each other in the center of the gallery like comrades in a war, taking in the devastation.

When I dug down for the courage to look at him and finally faced him, he was ashen, as pale as any one of my images on the wall.

He spoke to me, but he never once looked my way.

"You didn't tell me."

"I didn't know."

"You didn't know that you were going to his house and taking your clothes off every single day? Or you didn't know that I would be here today, still in the picture?"

He looked all around the gallery. I was so attuned to him I could hear his breath through the noise and the crowd. I could hear the air moving through his lungs. The blood running through his veins.

I was sure that if I listened hard enough I could hear his bone marrow making blood.

"There must be more than thirty paintings in here," he said.

"He worked fast. I wasn't there very often. I did not sit for these."

"He made them up?"

"No."

I could have lied but I didn't.

"He painted them from memory," I said.

"Even that one?" he asked, pointing to the one single canvas where Michael had included himself in the image. It was a painting of the two of us in the bathroom, him shaving my right leg, which was draped over the side of the marble tub, and me smoking a cigarette. The image was private, carefree, decadent, and damning. Michael had titled it *Lovers in the Bathroom.* I didn't know how Gabriel could ever come back from seeing it. I didn't know how our relationship would survive it.

"He made so many things," I said. "He painted suns and stars and children. I sat for him once. There was only one single portrait that I knew of. He did not tell me the show would look like this."

With every passing moment Gabriel looked more and more confused.

"I've been in the library day after day, working for our future," he said.

"I know."

"You know. You don't know. Which is it, Evangeline?"

The complete calmness of his voice frightened me to no end.

"Every night when I came home you seemed so mysterious," he said, "so sensual. I thought it was New Orleans. Maybe the heat and the beauty of the city had gotten to you. I thought that maybe you would stay here with me. I was naïve enough to think it was me that you wanted."

Gabriel laughed out loud.

"But it was Michael all along, wasn't it? It was never me at all. I should have listened to Madame Susteen when she told me that you would break my heart."

The gallery was shocking not just for the paintings themselves, but also for the scent of the rooms. Men and women walked around with their noses in the air like dogs at the beach trying to suss out a smell floating by on a current of air. Everyone thought it was a brilliant idea, a scented gallery, but no one figured out that it was coming from the paintings themselves. Women begged the gallery owner to tell them what the scent was, and she told them that she did not know. They thought she was being coy when really she was as baffled as they.

But Gabriel knew. He stood there by my side in silence. He didn't walk away and I thought that maybe the storm would not be as severe as I thought.

As it turned out I had a whole new talent for being wrong.

"How did he get it into the paint?" he asked.

I looked away from him and spoke with my head down. I told him the truth.

"My hair, my skin, and my nails."

"Is that why he's shaving your leg?" he asked, pointing at *Lovers in the Bathroom*.

"It is."

"He knew it would sell his paintings?"

"He did."

"And you agreed."

"I did."

"Do you think this is what Louise had in mind? Do you think she made this incredible scent for Michael Bon Chance? Is that what you think?"

"I don't know."

The images surrounded us, looming over us, drowning out anything I might have to say on my behalf. And what was there to say? How could I explain to Gabriel that I had been bewitched? That

Michael had woven a spell around me? How could I tell him that I wanted to give my scent to Michael—to anyone at all who would take it away?

Looking at the rooms full of images, my time with Michael captured forever in skin and fingernails and hair and paint, I was shocked at how sensual they were.

I did not have to turn around to know that Gabriel was gone.

52

I searched through the crowd until I found Michael. I grabbed his arm for support that I knew would be withheld.

"Ah, this is Evangeline," he said to the woman standing next to him in a pink column dress with a blond Chihuahua tucked under her arm.

"You must be thrilled," she said, clasping her palms together and bringing them to her chest in a pantomime of someone being thrilled.

"These are such exquisite pieces. Someday I would love to be the muse of a great artist. That's what you are, you know," she said, turning her gaze to Michael, "a great artist."

She handed him a business card.

"I'm ready to sit whenever you're ready to paint," she said over her shoulder as she walked into the crowd.

Michael turned to me.

"Did you hear what she called me? She said I was a great artist. Did you hear that? That's the first time anyone has ever said that to me, and it's because of you, Evangeline."

I ignored him.

"You tried to ruin Gabriel and me from the start, didn't you? That's why you took us to the Broken Heart Ballroom. It was a hint. A bit of fun and games, but you were the only one playing."

"Not now, Evangeline, please. Not today."

"When? When would be a good time for you, Michael?"

"Careful, your scent is starting to show. I don't want people to notice you."

I could not remember ever feeling this way before but I had to hold myself back, physically. If I'd had anything sharp in my hand, a pen, a bottle opener, a pair of scissors, there would have been blood on the gallery floor.

"I knew nothing back at the Broken Heart," he said. "Nothing was planned. I hadn't even met you yet."

"No, you had not, but Madame Susteen had. She's the one who told you about me and the scent on my body and how it might help your paintings. It was right after Gabriel and I met with her, wasn't it?"

The sentence was out of my mouth before I realized that it was true. It surprised both of us that I knew.

"We'll talk about it later, when we're celebrating all the money we're going to make. It will all be worth it, Evangeline, believe me."

He put his ice-cold hands around me as people snapped pictures of the two of us that were sure to show up in the papers the next day. Just one more thing that would be impossible to explain to Gabriel.

It seemed like a long, endless string of circumstances had been created to push Michael and me together. Everything from Louise's death in Cyril right up until this evening in the Royal Street gallery had condensed into this moment of fame for Michael and of destruction of love for Gabriel and me. It was as if something had to be taken apart for another thing to come together.

I watched as Michael was absorbed into the lustful arms of his new public. Red dots showed up on every painting in every room. Cries went up from the mesmerized crowd when the gallery owner asked everyone to be quiet and then announced that the show had sold out. People lined up to write large checks for the next works of Michael Bon Chance before brush ever touched canvas. I had underestimated him. He had accomplished his goal of working my scent into his once uninspired paintings.

I stood in the doorway taking one last look at the gallery before leaving. I watched Michael accept many congratulations and too much money with one eye always on his new patron and the other forever trained on me.

Outside the gallery dogs were barking furiously. Their owners had tied them up on the street while they viewed the artwork, and the combination of the scent from the canvases coming through the open French doors and the smell of my body as I stepped onto the sidewalk was too much for them. They struggled and pulled at their leashes just like the dogs that had lunged at me on the bank of the Mississippi River just weeks before.

I paused in memory for just a second too long, inciting a gray dog with a streak of white lightning down its back to break free and latch its pointy teeth onto my arm. I felt the fangs trying to break through my skin and coming dangerously close to the branching blue veins on my wrist. I tried to free my arm from its mouth. I looked up and down the street for help, but it was empty. Except for the dogs and Gabriel it seemed that every living thing in New Orleans was inside the gallery looking at my nude body.

Michael was the one who spotted me through the open window. He came outside and grabbed the dog by the jaws, pulling them apart until it let go of my wrist, until my arm fell out of its mouth like a piece of wood. He took a long white handkerchief out of the breast pocket of his suit and tied it tightly around the two small red puncture wounds on my arm. The dogs on their leashes looked tormented and struggled even harder.

He looked around him before whispering, "Don't leave without giving it back to me."

"You want the handkerchief? That's why you came out here to help me?" I said, my voice raspy with hate and desperation.

He began to untie the cloth but I held it tight.

"It's mine," I said. "I'm not giving you even one tiny drop of my blood."

"Give it to me," he said, and he tried to pull it off my wrist. "Do you know how many paintings I could make with that?"

I ripped myself free and ran away from him, down Royal Street, holding the cloth tight against my skin. I knew he would be torn between following me and collecting accolades from the strangers in the gallery and I was certain he would go for the immediate gratification of the fame and the glory. I was right; when I turned around his shape, while still outside, was getting smaller and smaller.

I thought about stopping in the supermarket for something antiseptic, but I heard dogs barking from behind the doors and iron gates up and down Royal Street, so I decided against it. The feral cats that were all over the French Quarter hissed and bared their vicious-looking fangs, so I walked home fast and every once in a while I looked over my shoulder for animals on the loose.

Back at the house I inspected the bite. There was no more blood, but redness and swelling had developed almost immediately. Liquid seeped from the puncture holes and dripped into the sink. The drop hitting the porcelain sounded like a boulder in my ear, and with a ferocious intensity, as though it was happening right at the moment, I remembered the sound of Gabriel's sweat striking the bottom of the white room in Louise's house. The rest of the blood in my body jumped and shuddered at the sound. I could tell because I saw the veins in my wrist rippling as if they had tiny ocean waves inside of them.

I needed to get to a pharmacy as soon as I could. I weighed my fear of going back outside against my need for first aid, and decided to knock on Levon's door instead. The mother of a teenaged boy would surely have what I needed.

53

Levon answered the door himself in the same white wife-beater and low-slung jeans he'd been wearing since I met him and I briefly wondered whether or not he had any other clothes. They looked clean enough, but I gave his surface only a quick gaze, as I was always wary of appearing to be looking too closely at his teenaged beauty.

"Evangeline, I was waiting for the day you would come over to my house," he said. "Want to come inside?"

"Is your mother home?"

"She's sleeping."

"I don't want to wake her up."

"Don't worry, nothing wakes her up. She sleeps like a dead person."

There was something chilly about Levon referring to his mother as a dead person, but I looked at my arm and went inside anyway.

The apartment was dominated by a large floor-to-ceiling credenza. Its doors were open and its interior shelves, which stretched along the entire back wall of the living room, were packed to the brim with odd objects and strange trinkets.

I got up close and saw things I wished I hadn't. Long ringlets of shiny black hair that looked recently oiled, held together with pink, sparkly ponytail holders. Silver forks with old, stiff food jammed between the prongs, sticky-looking medicine jars filled with brown, viscous liquids, a child's pink gymnastics bodysuit wrapped in a dirty tutu. There were wicker baskets filled with figurines and worthless-looking jewels, bundles of herbs, single shoes, voodoo beads, and ceramic body parts like the finger Levon had asked me to drop off at the cemetery.

"It's my old grandma's stuff," he said. "She calls it her cabinet of curiosities. She gave it to my mother as a birthday present."

Happy birthday to her, I thought.

"I like to look at them when she's not here so I don't miss her so much."

"Did you oil the hair?" I asked.

"I do it every Sunday so it doesn't dry out. I don't like it, but my old grandma is smart so I do what she says most of the time."

"My old grandma Louise was like that too."

"She died?"

"Yes. And I miss her every single day."

"How'd she die?"

"I'm not really sure."

"Oh, that's bad. That's the kind of thing you could think about forever. It could suck out all your energy."

"I've learned to live with it," I said.

"What happened to your arm?"

Even with his cabinet filled with ceramic body parts and hair I did not think Levon was ready for the story of Michael Bon Chance and the gallery show.

"I got bit by a dog," I said.

"You could get rabies."

"I thought about that myself, but I'm pretty sure it was someone's pet, so I doubt it."

"Don't touch me," he said.

"Don't worry, I won't."

"You want me to pull a card and see if you're gonna lose the hand?"

"I'm not going to lose my hand, Levon. I just need some alcohol or iodine."

He looked over at the cabinet of curiosities.

"Not from there," I said. "I'm not using something your old grandma left you to clean on Sundays."

"You'd be surprised how powerful some of that stuff is."

"You'd be surprised how fast I can run out of here."

"Okay, let me check the bathroom," he said.

"Thank you."

I turned from the strange cabinet in the living room, and looked into Levon's kitchen. It looked like an old Laundromat with clothes hung on thick strands of white rope crisscrossing the room like a child's game of Jacob's ladder.

There was a washing board in the kitchen sink, the ribbed kind that people used to rub their clothes on before washing machines were invented. The apartment smelled like laundry detergent and mold, as if the curio cabinet and the clean clothes were fighting for domination of the senses.

Levon came back and walked into the kitchen, ducking his head under the jeans, T-shirts, and underwear strung over the lines.

"Why don't you hang this stuff outside in the sunlight?" I said. "Over the railing on the balcony? It would dry a lot quicker."

"Cause of the ravens," said Levon. "My old grandma says it's terrible luck if a raven flies over your clothes. She says whenever you wear them bad things will happen to your body. I believe her too. I used to hang my mama's clothes outside in the courtyard and one day she got hit by a car, and her leg and her arm were never good again. That's why she sleeps all the time."

"Arthritis?"

"That's right. She got the arthritis."

"You think it was a raven that did it?"

"I only washed her pants and her shirt and she only hurt her leg and her arm. Her clothes were hexed by the bird. Since then I don't hang anything outside. I don't even hang clothes next to the window. A raven has excellent eyesight and can easily spot your clothes and bust through your window with its beak."

"You do all the laundry by yourself?"

"And I read the cards. I got a gift in both of those fields. I got the second sight and a strong washing arm. My mama says I'll never be poor."

Levon flexed the muscle of his arm as he handed me a bottle of rubbing alcohol.

"If it doesn't work, come back and we'll try something from the cabinet. You sure you don't want me to turn over a card for you while you're here?"

"No thanks, Levon. I still have the Magician. I'll bring it back to you later."

"Don't keep it too long or everything in your life's gonna go in reverse. Big to small, up to down, forward to backward. That's the way the Magician works."

54

Back in my own kitchen I spread the bite marks apart with my fingers to see what was inside but it was too dark to get a good view. I aimed the bottle of alcohol directly at the holes and poured. I took the sharp, stinging pain as yet another punishment for what I had done to Gabriel. I emptied the bottle on my arm and then wrapped it with a dishtowel hanging over the handle of the stove.

Gabriel did not come home that night and I wasn't surprised, but I sat up for a long time in bed listening for the sound of his feet on the stairs. He walked slowly when he was carrying a lot of books and fast when he was carrying a lot of books but still couldn't wait to climb into bed next to me. I wondered whether he would ever feel that way again. At five o'clock in the morning I finally fell asleep, my wrist throbbing with pain.

When I woke up, the sun was shining and the sprinklers were on over the garden. The drops hitting the big, sturdy leaves of the banana plants were irritating, but the sprinkler system was controlled by the building and I had no way to shut it off on my own.

I turned to Gabriel's side of the bed and ran my hands over the pillow searching for a dent that maybe I could feel but not see, but there was none. I felt the blanket, perfectly smooth with no warmth. No chance that he had come and gone in the middle of the night while I slept.

I checked for water in the bathroom sink. It was bone dry, but that's when I noticed that his toothbrush was gone. At first I felt relieved that he had been in the house, but then I felt panic that he had taken his toothbrush. It was amazing how many emotions were inspired by the loss of a blue plastic stick with white bristles.

I checked the kitchen and the living room. They were oddly still, as if without Gabriel there was no one home. As if the apartment itself had discounted me because of my actions.

One side effect of my search for signs of him, of the intense focus on the possible displacement of small things, was that the pain in my wrist felt temporarily better. The act of searching, more than alcohol or antiseptic cream, seemed to be the solution to my pain. Maybe if I kept on going, searching for him day and night, my entire life would become pain free.

I gave up and lay down on the couch in the living room. Running from room to room had caused me to sweat and the scent coming out of me was extreme. It was beautiful enough to make me forget my troubles momentarily and love myself at least until I cooled off, which in Louisiana could take a while.

I stretched my legs and arranged a pillow under my head, fanned out my hair so it wouldn't stick to the sweat on the back of my neck, and closed my eyes.

A picture of Michael came into my mind and I could not get it out. Without realizing it, I had gotten used to being touched and shaved and groomed and painted during the day. My body felt aroused and unloved. I tried to focus on where Gabriel could be and whether or not he would return, but the thought of Michael was an inescapable constant.

I looked out the window at the vines growing all along the walls of the building and I felt that maybe Michael had planted something inside of me, like a weed that was also attached to him. I felt listless and restless at the same time. As if I wanted to leap off the couch, but was nailed to it.

Sometime later I got up and went to check the closet where Gabriel kept his clothes. I held the knob in my hand before turning it. Inside would be the answer to my question. I felt as if the doorknob held my fate and I hated it for the power it had over me. When it finally turned, Gabriel's things were still inside. At least I thought they were. I didn't know every item of his clothing—we hadn't known each other long enough for that—but the piles that I had formed while he was at the library looked to be about the same size as they usually were.

I thought the sight of his T-shirts and jeans still in place might give me peace, but they didn't. I knew it was not a question of his wanting to leave them behind, it was simply that he'd had no time to collect them.

I went upstairs into the bedroom in search of his backpack and textbooks, and those, as I'd feared, were gone. I counted the things he had carried away: a backpack, somewhere around ten books, and a toothbrush.

I lay on the bed, tired as if I'd run a marathon, even though I'd only climbed a single flight of stairs. I closed my eyes and immediately thought of Michael once again. It seemed that the only way to shut him out of my head was to keep my eyes open, so I lay there, exhausted, staring at the ceiling.

I was focusing on the antique light fixture when I realized the true nature of my problem. It was annoying and clichéd that I was looking at a lightbulb when I had my big idea, but there it was. So, it was not what I had done, the leg shavings and the nail clippings and the haircuts. Those were bad, they were, and I knew that, but they were not the real problem. If I was honest with myself the real problem was that I didn't know who made me happy, Gabriel or Michael.

Maybe I *was* happy with Michael and his all-consuming passion and dedication to his work. Or maybe it was the steadfastness of Gabriel that I really wanted. Either way, my problem was not that I'd sat for those paintings and wronged Gabriel. It was much worse than that. It was that I did not know what I felt. And the reason I didn't know was that both of these men were connected to this scent, which was not me. Not the real, born-with-it me, anyway.

55

The phone rang like a fire alarm. I ran down the stairs and grabbed the receiver.

"We sold all thirty paintings with commissions for a dozen more."

"Michael?"

"I have to make more paint, Evangeline. Just do this one last thing for me and I promise I will not ask you for anything ever again. I'll split my profits with you. I'll give you the apartment for free. Whatever you want."

"Don't call here, Michael."

"You agreed to do this with me," he said. "You can't back out now. We have to finish what we started."

I felt confused.

"I can't see you right now."

"Take my word on it," he said, "time apart will only make my heart grow violent."

I hung up the phone. Could I love a man with a violent heart?

Maybe if I found out what was in Louise's vial I could have it made and give it to him and then he would leave me alone. But until that happened I was sure he would hound me. I was the key to his fame and he had wound his mind around my skin like a vine.

I went back upstairs to bed. The phone rang and rang all morning. I knew I did not have much time before Michael arrived at the apartment, which was technically his own, but I didn't know where else to go.

At the next ring I faced my fate and answered.

"Evangeline?"

"Yes?"

"It's Levon. Your neighbor."

I exhaled a long, smooth breath.

"Have you been calling here?"

"Yes."

"Why didn't you come over like you always do?"

"I was worried about you," he said. "I wanted to know how your hand was but I didn't want to bother you in case you were in bed sleeping."

"That's very nice of you, Levon. I'm doing just fine."

"I called my old grandma. She says to come and see her anytime. She'll fix up your hand free of charge 'cause you're a friend of mine."

"Tell her thank you. But I'm okay, really."

"If you change your mind, let me know."

I hung up the phone and checked on my wrist. I unwrapped the dishtowel and I was upset at the sight of the wound. There was a kind of ooze coming out of it. Two strange leaking holes on an otherwise perfect arm. I covered them up like a secret from myself, with a brand-new T-shirt. I had a closet full of them now that Gabriel was gone.

56

Levon's friend Roger drove us to out to Bayou Jolie on the Atchafalaya Basin, to see Levon's old grandma.

Just my luck, his pickup truck was exactly like my mother's car, a gray tank with roll-down windows and a Tahitian girl in a grass skirt hanging from the rearview mirror. I felt like I was home even though I was getting farther away with each passing minute.

Roger wore a cut-off T-shirt. He had thick biceps, a sly smile, and an American flag bandanna tied around his head. A long blond sun-bleached ponytail hung down his back. He didn't say a lot but he tossed my bag into the back as if it were light as a lollipop stick.

"Ready to roll?" he asked.

I got in the front seat while Levon lay out in the back, his head against one window, his feet propped up against the other.

"How did you two meet?" I asked.

Roger had to be twenty-five years older than Levon, and it was hard to see the connection in any way that was legal.

"We don't know each other," said Roger.

I turned away and looked out the window. I stared at the Mississippi to my right and tried to shut out Roger's sentence. Here we go again, I thought. I sat up a little straighter in my seat and made sure the door was unlocked in case I needed to jump out at the next light.

"I'm a friend of Vivian Weaver," he continued as we pulled onto the interstate. "Levon's grandmother. I run errands for her and she fixes my back when it goes out. It's been a problem since I started driving a semi a while back. It's the lower part, the lumbar spine, they call it. I call it a pain in the butt. It's got a dull throb that drives me crazy on long hauls, but when Vivian Weaver gets her hands on it I get two, maybe three good days."

"So this is an errand?"

"Yep. She said her grandson had a friend who needed a drive out to the bayou, so here I am."

"What do you haul?" I asked.

"Cattle, mostly. The kind of trucking that gives me a chance to get out of the South and over to livestock country in the Midwest. I like the wide-open spaces. I was born in Louisiana but it's a pretty tight place compared to the middle of the country. Hot and swampy too. A man can't get any privacy in the South."

He spit a wad of chewing tobacco out the window.

"Don't get me wrong, I love it here, I love it like my own mother. It is my own mother, but it's good to get away from your mother every once in a while too."

I felt closer to Roger the longer he talked and I agreed with most of the things he said.

"How long is the trip to Bayou Jolie?" I asked.

"Oh, not long. Two or three hours at most. You tired already?"

"Nope, not yet."

The truth was I felt like I could stay in the truck with the wind on my face forever. It went up my nostrils and blew through my eyelashes. It held my hair tight against my head like a barrette and for at least one moment it blew my guilt about Gabriel right out onto the highway and turned it into roadkill.

The longer the trip went on, the more Roger seemed like a straight-up kind of guy. He told me everything he knew about the Atchafalaya Basin, about its being located in South Central Louisiana, and how it's the largest swamp in the country where the Atchafalaya River meets the Gulf of Mexico. He never veered off into weirdo territory like most of the people I'd met so far. Nothing unusual. Not a tarot card, a lock of hair, or a ceramic body part in sight. I tilted my seat back and watched the tall swamp grass go by.

"Mind if I smoke?" he asked.

"Not at all."

"You mind, boy?" he yelled to Levon over the roar of a passing truck. I turned around and saw that Levon was sleeping.

"He fell fast," I said. "Probably the motion. I used to sleep like that when I was a kid."

"Nah. It ain't the movement," said Roger. "If I was a bettin' man I'd put money on it that his grandmother did that to him. You know, put it in his mind from far away that he ought to rest awhile before he gets out to Jolie."

I didn't enter into that conversation with Roger. It was just the kind of talk I wanted to avoid. Moments before we'd moved away from the story of the swamplands and onto the history of the Cajun people. He had just finished telling me how Joseph Broussard led the first group of some two hundred Acadians from Canada to Louisiana in 1765 on a boat called the *Santo Domingo,* and right then that was all I wanted to hear. Nothing about Levon's grandmother putting a spell on him from a distance.

Roger looked at my wrist, neatly wrapped with a maroon pillowcase I'd cut in half. I used a dark color to cover up any sticky substance that might leak out of the bite.

"I've been meaning to ask, is that why you're going to see Vivian Weaver?"

"It's a dog bite," I said. "I was bitten a couple of days ago and I don't think it's healing right."

Roger stiffened in his seat. He rolled down his window as far as it would go, spat twice, and patted himself on his left shoulder with his right hand.

"New Orleans can be a tough town, but I gotta tell you, no matter where you are, dog bites are never a good sign. When man's best friend turns against you, you can bet you've got a serious problem. In fact, I'd put money on it you did something wrong. Maybe even something heinous."

"You put money on a lot of things, don't you?"

"Never mind that," he said. "What did you do, girl? We got a long trip ahead of us, and no radio reception. Perfect time for talking."

"I want to hear more about the Atchafalaya Basin," I said.

"All right," he said, laughing. "Didn't mean to spook you. Let me see what I can remember. I knew all of this by heart at one time, but I was a real young man then. It's a pity my mind's not what it used to be."

I stared out the window and concentrated on trying to forget that Roger's mind was not what it used to be. What did that mean? Were we going to veer off the road and into the basin? Or was he going to forget the way to Levon's old grandma Vivian Weaver's house?

"Okay, I'll tell you what," he said. "I know there's a wildlife refuge out there that people from up east pay a lot of money to visit. They muck around in the swamps with their high boots and their gloves and their expensive camera equipment hoping to see a gator or some nesting cranes. Thing is, they're so busy protecting all that gear, half the time they miss what they came all the way out here to see."

Roger laughed. I glanced over at him and saw a set of extra-long teeth with brown tobacco stains. The yellow fang on the side of his front tooth looked like it belonged to a vicious animal in the rodent family. I pictured him ripping into one of those cattle he hauled across the country, with his bare teeth.

"There are a lot of bayous," he continued, "cypress swamps and marshes, that type of thing. The basin is prone to flood, so not many people stick to living in the area. They come out here with high hopes, adventurous sorts, all of 'em, but they almost always leave. Some folks end up liking it, though, high water and all. People like Vivian Weaver seem to thrive out here. She was born way over in Evangeline Parish. I have no idea how she came to live in Jolie, but she's been there a long time and folks depend on her abilities."

"Evangeline Parish?"

"Yep, same as your name. Pretty name. I'm surprised her grandson never told you?"

I looked back at Levon, still sleeping. Maybe Vivian Weaver *had* put a spell on him.

"What are her special abilities?" I asked.

"You'll have to wait and see for yourself," Roger said, and then he did what I feared most and put his big right hand on my knee. I thought that between the open windows, the cigarette smoke, and the diesel fumes from passing trucks, I'd be safe, but there I was with his fingers wrapping themselves around my thigh, burrowing in like a small animal trying to go home.

I felt my heart pick up speed. He was a big man and maybe I would never be able to get him off me. Maybe his hand would disappear right into my leg and become part of my blood supply.

"I was bitten by a dog, remember," I said. "I've got terrible luck."

He took his hand off me and put it back on the steering wheel without much fuss.

"A man gets lonely on the road," he said. "And you sure do smell good."

57

By 8:30 the sky was dark red, as if we were driving straight toward a bayou on Mars.

"They call it the bloodscent," said Roger. "When the sky turns that color insects and animals come out in droves, especially the ones that lust after the smell of blood. The mosquitoes, the biting flies, chiggers, gnats, gators, and wolverines and wolves—rougarous, they call them around here."

Not wanting to attract anything negative toward the car with my own scent, I rolled up the window. It was a risk shutting myself in like that because I didn't want to attract Roger either, but at that moment he seemed the safer option.

"How long till we get to Vivian Weaver's house?"

"Not long now," he said. "But it won't be any better over there. We're still gonna be looking at the sunset. Same problems. Same biters."

"What do you usually do when the sky turns this color?"

"Me, I stay inside my house. If I'd a known there was gonna be a bloodscent tonight, I'd never have driven the two of you out here. Now I'm gonna have to go all the way back home, alone, windows all rolled up tight with one eye on the road and the other on the rearview mirror. I hope this trip is worth your while and you get what you came out here for."

"You're not staying at Vivian Weaver's?"

"I wasn't invited. Are you inviting me?"

"I can't do that. I never met the woman."

"You're gonna let me risk my life driving out here late at night after a sunset like this? Do you know that a car went off this very highway not five years ago under a sky as red as this one? The body of the driver was found ripped to pieces. They said it was coyote, but I know it was a rougarou. A werewolf. I'm not a superstitious sort, but ain't no coyote in the world could make a man look like that."

"You could stay at a hotel."

"This is the Atchafalaya Basin, sweetheart. You see any hotels around here?"

"I guess not."

"You don't like me much, do you?" he said. "Maybe you're a tiny bit afraid of me 'cause I put my hand on your leg."

I didn't like this conversation much, that was for sure.

"I think you're just fine," I said.

"Well, I'm not so sure I like you right about now. You better just be careful or I could make a wrong turn and the three of us'll be swamp meat in no time."

"You wouldn't do that to yourself," I said.

"I don't like myself much, Miss Evangeline. And for that reason I don't put anything past myself either."

That was a real conversation ender if I ever heard one. There was nowhere to go after a statement like that, so I sat back, prayed for Levon to wake up, hoping he hadn't been poisoned by Roger way back in New Orleans, and watched the bloodred sunset deepen over the Atchafalaya Basin.

۲٫

"It's really red out here," said Levon, speaking his first words in two and a half hours.

I turned and looked at him in the backseat.

"Your old grandma had better be worth it," I said.

"This is where I let you off," said Roger. "This is where the road ends."

"Right here? We're in the middle of nowhere," I said.

"The boy knows where to go."

"I don't," said Levon. "Last time I was here I was twelve years old. That was about a billion years ago. I don't remember anything anymore."

Roger rearranged the bandanna on his head, tightened the knot, and ran his hands down his ponytail.

"I don't want to see old Vivian Weaver right now. We had a little falling-out the last time and we haven't seen each other since. I agreed to do this one favor for her, because I owe her due to her fixing my back, but I don't think either of us much wants to see the other."

"Walk us to her place and then you can go," I said. "You don't have to come inside."

Roger and Levon both laughed at this.

"You don't know anything about Vivian Weaver. She probably knows I'm standing here talking about her. She probably knows exactly what I'm saying right now."

"My old grandma's a *traiteur*," said Levon. "She's a healer."

The wound had seemed to get worse on the trip. It leaked onto the torn piece of pillowcase so persistently it was as if something inside of me was trying to get out.

"She's not that kind of healer you're used to," said Roger. "She's a faith healer. She heals with prayer."

I leaned against the truck.

"She's going to pray for me?"

"She sure is."

I felt defeated. I knew that Vivian Weaver could not heal my arm with her faith. I tried picturing Louise in my mind but the vision of her did no good. Standing there under the red sunset I felt for the first time that she was really gone. Dead. A wolf howled in the distance, agreeing with me, sounding a mourning call over the death of Louise that echoed across the basin.

"It's getting dark," said Levon. "We better start walking."

"Vivian's farm is about a mile from here straight across this grassland. We should be able to make it before total darkness sets in," said Roger.

The three of us set out in single file. There was a loneliness to Bayou Jolie. A melancholy feeling that came from the redness and the silence that reminded me of the Broken Heart Ballroom.

"Don't let it get to you," said Roger. "Dusk is the most difficult time for us humans to be outside in the wilderness. I avoid it like the plague most days. It gives me the depressions. Makes me feel like crying and doing nothing else ever again."

Levon said his skin felt itchy, my wrist throbbed and leaked, and I could tell that Roger's mind was tense.

"We're lucky it's a clear night out here," he said, "otherwise we'd have to contend with lightning. You'd be on your own if that was the case. No way I'd be walking in an open field like this one."

"Did you ever meet anyone who was struck?" asked Levon.

"I knew a man once," said Roger. "A construction worker with a hard hat and a tool belt. He was hit somewhere near the western levee of the swamp while putting up a phone line. After the strike his hat was permanently sealed onto his scalp. Looked like he had a giant orange head."

58

Vivian Weaver's house stood alone on the edge of nowhere. An old cypress farmhouse with two weatherboard cabins on either side, "for storage," said Levon. There was a tractor sitting out front in the moonlight, and by the height of the grass I could tell it had not been used all season. There was no smoke coming out of the chimney and no lights on in the house. I wondered if she was still alive or if we were going to open the door and find a dried-out, dusty corpse with bones that turned to ash at the slightest touch.

"Don't worry, she's in there," said Roger, as if he were reading my mind. "She likes to pray in the dark and this is the time of night she practices her faith."

Levon hesitated, and then knocked on the wooden frame of the screen door.

His hesitation was not a comfort.

We waited in silence until Vivian Weaver stepped into the doorway and beckoned us with her finger from the other side of the screen.

"Come on in, children. Come on," she said, her index finger hooked toward herself like a claw. "Let me turn on the light so I can get a better look at my beautiful grandson."

The light she referred to turned out to be a 15-watt bulb that illuminated nothing.

I turned to Roger but he was nowhere in sight. I looked out behind me onto the field but it was too dark to see. I wished him well in my mind and hoped no harm would come to him alone out there in the disappearing bloodscent sunset.

"Roger's long gone," said Vivian Weaver. "Don't look for him now. He has it in his mind that we don't care for one another anymore. Of course he's wrong. He doesn't care for me, but I love him like a son."

"I think he's afraid of you," I said.

"Well then, that's a problem, because it's hard to love someone you're afraid of," she answered.

Vivian Weaver was not at all what I expected. She was neat and clean and looked as if she had just come home from a day at the beauty parlor. Her black-and-gray hair had a fresh roller-set look; the front portion came up and off her face. She had dark eyes and wore bright red lipstick. Her black dress was neat and long sleeved. It buttoned up the front and came down below her knees. She had a tissue tucked into the sleeve and sensible, square-toed, low-heeled shoes. If I had to guess, I'd say she was somewhere in her late seventies or early eighties.

"I've heard a lot about you," I said. "Levon never stops talking about you."

"I know you're thinking that I'm too old to have a grandson his age," she said. "But I was one of those lucky women who had an accidental pregnancy very late in life. I was well over fifty years old when I had his mother. It wasn't a difficult time either. I barely knew I was pregnant. In fact, for the first five months I thought I was going through the change of life."

Vivian Weaver, like most old people I knew, like Rosemary, in fact, lacked inhibition when it came to talking about her life. It was as if social mores were eventually acknowledged as a waste of time and precious energy as a person got older.

Levon put his arms around his grandmother and the resemblance was unmistakable. He had blond hair and she black, but it was in the eyes. Long and dark, starting out narrow near the nose and getting wider and slanting upward toward the outside, the way alien eyes look in the movies.

"You're going to have a late pregnancy too," she said, "but yours is going to be difficult. Not at all like my own. There's going to be a lot of blood and pain and all sorts of unnameable problems."

Of course, I thought. Of course there will be.

"Come, come, no need to think about it now," she said. "Let me show you the rest of the house."

Aside from the all-pervasive darkness the house was the same as Vivian Weaver herself—that is to say it was unremarkable to look at. The living room had a couch with a bright floral print and two chairs of the same fabric, all covered in plastic as if to prevent them from aging the way she had. There was a dark wooden breakfront with a set of dishes, and a dining-room table for eight. Nothing even the slightest bit out of the ordinary except for the fact that rosaries and candles, depictions of the Virgin Mary and the archangels were everywhere, although in this very Catholic part of Louisiana that probably wasn't unusual at all.

I thought about the cabinet of curiosities that she had given to Levon's mother with the locks of oily hair, the dirty ballerina dress, and the old utensils covered in ancient food, and I could not put those things together with the small, neat woman in front of me who covered her sofa in plastic. Maybe she kept all her strangeness at the apartment in New Orleans with Levon and his mother. That was fine with me. I felt relaxed, almost sleepy, in her presence and then, suddenly, out of nowhere, totally alert, as Vivian Weaver's absolute normalcy began to terrify me.

59

Vivian Weaver took us from pot to pot in her kitchen, lifting lids, stirring and tasting as she went along. There was seafood gumbo, fried fish and fried chicken, dumplings, butter biscuits, cornbread, fried okra, black-eyed peas, green beans, and bread pudding.

Levon sat down and ate as if he had just been on a forty-mile hike instead of a two-hour drive. He ate the way only a teenaged boy can. It was so fascinating to watch that I almost forgot about my own food. He took a break, fork in the air, mouth full, and looked at me with pleading eyes that went from my plate to my mouth. I understood that I was being rude to Vivian Weaver. I started eating right away, not willing to run the risk of inciting her dislike.

When Levon was full, he leaned over and whispered in my ear, "Ask her to look at your hand."

"She doesn't know about it?"

"Of course she does, she's old, not blind. But she's a *traiteur*. You have to ask for her help. She can't offer it unless you beg. It's part of the gig."

"I'm not begging."

"Beg," he said and then he panted like a dog.

"Mrs. Weaver," I began.

"Vivian Weaver," she said.

"Vivian Weaver," I said, feeling odd having to call her by her entire name, "I have a bite on my wrist that doesn't seem to be healing. Do you think you can help me?"

Levon panted harder.

"I can try, sweetheart. But first I need you to tell me the story of your life leading right up to the bite that won't heal."

· "The whole thing?"

"Well, not the whole thing. I'll be dead before you can tell me all that. Just the important things. And don't leave out the part about how you got that scent that's clinging to you so tenaciously."

"I'm sorry. I would have mentioned it, but I thought your cooking, which by the way is more than delicious, would cover it."

"Honey, a dead animal couldn't cover that up. Now go on before I fall asleep. I'm all ears, but I haven't got too many years."

She rocked back and forth just a little bit, laughing at her own joke.

I told her the story from New York City to Cyril to New Orleans. I told her about Louise and the vial and Gabriel. I told her how I came to meet Michael, and I admitted to what happened between us. And then I told her about the dogs outside the gallery.

"Hmmm," said Vivian Weaver. "And I was pretty darn sure I'd heard everything by now."

"Can you help me?"

"I can tell you that being involved with evil is what caused your predicament."

"I'm not sure I would call Michael evil."

"You better be sure. Feeling the ambiguities leads to feeling the pain. I was in a similar situation to the one you describe at one time in my life. I was involved with a man named Señor Malpito. He was the worst man I ever knew. He beat me senseless twice in one year and he wasn't even drunk. Nope. He was stone-cold sober. One morning he finished his coffee, wiped his face with a napkin, and then went to business on *my* face. Well, of course I had to get myself out of that situation, and I did, but I'll tell you the truth, I missed the old son of a bitch after he was gone. I miss him to this day, and I'm not embarrassed about it. Not one bit. I said my farewells to him in a dream, the saddest dream I ever had. Believe me, it can be hard to say goodbye to a bad man too."

"That's just how I feel."

"Let's all say goodbye to Señor Malpito," she said.

"Goodbye, Señor Malpito," the three of us said.

"A goodbye is a goodbye is a goodbye," she said. "And none of them are good. Some people will tell you that it's smart to get rid of certain folks in your life, but I've lived a long time and I think every goodbye leaves a scar. I don't like the whole damn business."

"I don't either," I said.

As I stood in the kitchen listening to Vivian Weaver I was sure that I should, at that very moment, be sitting in a doctor's office back in the Quarter, or better yet in New York City. It wasn't that I didn't think she could help, it was just that my hand seemed to be getting worse by the minute, and I didn't want to "lose it," as Levon had said I might, back in New Orleans.

"I'm considered a good doctor in these parts, Evangeline," said Vivian Weaver. "I can cure all sorts of ailments and I have an excellent track record. Earaches, toothaches, angina, headaches, bleeding disorders, stomach pains, warts, shingles, and the asthma too. The only thing I won't go near is sunstroke. All that heat coming out of the body makes me woozy. Sets me back for days. But other than that I've seen it all and I've cured it all. And don't you worry, I work with medicinal remedies as well as the laying on of hands, and the Lord himself. How many doctors do you know who can do all that? The spirit is my ace in the hole, so to speak. An added bonus that no regular doctor is going to give you. In fact, a lot of them take that part away and make the patient sicker than they really have to be. Remember to tell that to your friend Doctor Gabriel."

"You think I'll see Gabriel again?"

"I will have you up and running in no time and then you can make the choices you need to make."

"I'm not good at making decisions."

"You came here, didn't you?"

"That was Levon's decision."

"Well, you listened to the right person. Levon is very intelligent, in case you haven't noticed. He's much smarter than either you or I. I would pass down what I know about healing but he's already way past me. Most days I'm waiting for him to teach me something."

⌇

Vivian Weaver began to walk away toward the back of the farm-house, but she turned around midway down the hall.

"Let me take a closer look at that hand before I go to bed."

"It's late. If you want to start in the morning I can wait another night."

"Now is a better time. The light's not too good, so I can get a feel for the problem without having to look at it. An intuition, if you will."

I looked at Levon and he shrugged his shoulders.

"Can't hurt," he said.

"That's my boy. Now come over to the sink, young lady, and let me get that stinking thing cleaned up."

Vivian Weaver's voice had changed so much with the word "stinking" that even Levon looked startled.

She lit a candle and held it over my wrist.

"Deep puncture wounds. Two fangs. Three inches apart. Nope. That was no ordinary dog that bit you. No dog I know has fangs that far apart."

She wrapped the wound and took my old dirty maroon pillow-case.

"I'm going to sleep on this."

"Michael used to do that; take things covered in my body fluids."

"He's a trapped man, that one. I knew it the moment you told me about all those water nymphs he painted on the walls of his studio. Is he from New Orleans originally?"

"Born and raised."

"The people here are born below the sea level and they spend their whole lives wanting to go back to where they came from. My own theory is that everyone from here was a mermaid in another lifetime and they are all trying to swim back to the bottom of the ocean. That Michael of yours will drag you down to the depths if you let him. It's not his fault either. That's where he's most comfortable."

رب

I followed Vivian Weaver as she walked through the house sprinkling holy water in every room she passed.

"We're a superstitious people here on the bayou" was all she would say, and by the time we got to my bedroom I was glad that she was not more conversational.

The room was large and empty except for a four-poster bed and a framed picture of Marie Laveau, the voodoo queen of New Orleans.

"A free woman of color who owned her own business," said Vivian Weaver. "She made her own money, and rose to fame and power in a segregated South. Can you imagine such a thing? You're lucky to be sleeping in the same room with her."

60

That night as I lay down to sleep my arm was worse than ever. It was swollen, and hot, like a desert wind.

I reached into the darkness and searched through my small bag for the tiny vial that had held the scent Louise had made. I held it close and asked Louise to please help me make sense of the negative turn my life had taken.

With the ruby glass on my chest I dreamed of her. She sat on the edge of the bed and for a long while I got lost in staring at her face. Not wanting to let her go I reached out and touched her skin and her lips and her tall pile of fine gray hair. Finally, with great reluctance, I stopped touching her and listened to her words instead.

She spoke to me in soft tones that I strained to hear and might have missed if she had not repeated them so many times. I opened my eyes to write them down and the world seemed full of shadows and shifting shapes. As I adjusted to the darkness I could see that it was not Louise who was sitting on the edge of my bed, whose face I was touching, whose words I was listening to, but Vivian Weaver herself, leaning over my body, a spectral form in the middle of the night speaking to me in a singsong voice, repeating lines like a child's rhyme and holding my wounded wrist to her heart.

> *There are scents that linger long,*
> *and in the right proportion*
> *bring love and wishes and mighty song*
> *to those with true devotion.*
> *Do not try to mix and pry if you should lose this potion,*
> *for each soul only one drop exists,*
> *to set your love in motion.*

"It's time to set your true love in motion," she whispered. "Finish what you started, Evangeline."

I sat up in bed and freed my hand from hers.

"Tell me what you mean, Vivian Weaver."

And in her high child's voice she sang another poem.

> *I am your mother,*
> *I can make you a brother.*
> *I'm not in your mind,*
> *I don't exist in your soul,*
> *But you will come to know me,*
> *You will feel it in your bones.*

"I don't understand."

"Try not to speak," she said. "I'm healing you now."

I looked down. I could not see my wrist in the dark but I could still feel its sickness and heat.

"Tell me what you mean, Vivian Weaver, please tell me."

And then she spoke the words I feared the most.

"Go back to Michael Bon Chance," she said. "Give him everything and you will free yourself forever. Give him nothing and you will be tied to him for eternity."

I felt my fingernails and stroked my hair in the darkness. I could offer him those parts of my body for the rest of my life. They would continue to grow and he would take them over and over again in a cycle of desperation without end.

"It will never be enough for him," I said.

I could envision myself spending my life in the French Quarter, feeding his need and making him famous while I grew old and then died in the lilac Victorian on Magazine Street.

"You are a part of his loop," said Vivian Weaver. "You helped to create him. You made him what he is and now you must finish what you started. If you don't he will live inside of you, tormenting you with a ceaseless, remorseless inner voice of pleading that not even the cries of your own child will be able to cover."

The thought of Michael living inside my mind made me weep right there in the bed.

"Forget about your nails and your hair," she said. "Those things are nothing but a weak and temporary fix that will not satisfy him in the longer term. Give him your blood, Evangeline, and then you will be free."

"My blood?"

"The very essence of you. It will be enough to sustain him. You'll see. And don't worry about dying. The spirit won't kill you unless it believes that it's your time. And in that case, you won't have a choice either way."

I could not fathom any reason Louise would have for bringing me to such a place as this and to such a conversation as the one I was in right now with Vivian Weaver. So strange were her words that I could barely get the next sentence out of my mouth.

"Why would the spirit think I should die?"

"Maybe you have a death wish sitting deep inside of you. Or the spirit might need you for other things—maybe has other plans for you that do not include remaining on this earth."

61

Vivian Weaver made the sign of the cross with my hand on her body. She prayed for me in the Cajun French of Bayou Jolie. I did not understand most of her words except for *Dieu est amour,* God is love, which she said over and again, in a voice low and soothing like a lullaby, and just when I was about to fall back asleep she began again.

"He will bleed you dry if you let him," she said. "For sure he will try. But remember that you have in your presence a doctor of the dead."

"Gabriel?"

"Gabriel will save you. Gabriel will heal you. He will take you places in love that you never imagined existed."

Vivian Weaver repeated the words of Father Madrid's sermon from what seemed like so long ago it could not possibly have taken place just months before.

"Try to remember," she said, "that pain is natural and it is there to be suffered and treated. It is unavoidable and best not thought of as separate from the rest of your life. Christ suffered for our sins but also to show us that suffering is human."

"Am I going to suffer?"

"Most likely you will."

"And Michael Bon Chance? What will happen to him?"

"Don't waste your energy thinking about him. He will take enough of it without your help. All you need to know is that if you do not give him everything he needs he will be the bane of your existence. A monkey on your back. Lice in your hair. Termites in your house. He will search for you wherever you are. If you go to the supermarket, he will be there. If you go to the theater, he will be there too. Eventually he will kill you for what you have." Vivian Weaver took a deep breath. "Or perhaps he will make you produce a child that he can use in the same way as he uses you."

"You mean he would force me?"

Vivian Weaver shrugged her shoulders.

"You need to go back to New Orleans to settle things with Mr. Bon Chance. But after that, you must leave Louisiana as quickly as possible and never come back. You cannot think about him or you will draw him to where you are no matter how far away from him that may be. You must train your mind against all thought of him. He feels that he can't survive without you, and believe me he will do whatever it takes to bring you close.

"I'll give you a prayer to say every day to help keep him out of your path, but even if you give him your soul, there are no guarantees."

"Can I ask you a question, Vivian Weaver? Why am I so attracted to him?"

"Because he is the key to knowing who you are. Without him, there is no you."

62

"Pray every day," called Vivian Weaver, waving goodbye from behind the screen door. "And remember, *Dieu est amour,* not Michael or even Gabriel." Then she hurried down the dirt path toward Levon and me.

"I almost forgot to tell you." Vivian Weaver took my arm, walked me off of the path and onto the grass and whispered in my ear.

"You need to take Levon with you when you go back to New York. He's yours now. I'm too old to take proper care of such a young boy."

"What about his mother? Who's going to take care of her?"

"Levon doesn't have a mother, sweetheart, she's long dead. I'm his only kin. He makes up that story about his mother so he can continue to live in New Orleans, unencumbered by adults. Otherwise someone would surely take him away and put him in a home somewhere or make him live with me, and he doesn't want to be out here in the sticks. Levon is a city boy at heart."

"How long has he lived alone?"

"He's never alone. I communicate with him every day. He hears me wherever I am. Plus I taught him the cards, so he has a trade. A gift really, but a trade as well."

"So he says."

"He likes you. He talks to you. The winds don't get in the way when it comes to you."

Levon and his curly winds had blown me all the way out to the Bayou Jolie to cure my hand. He would be coming back to Cyril. I didn't have to say anything to Vivian Weaver, she already knew.

"I'll bring him to visit sometime."

"No you won't. You can't come here anymore, remember?"

"I'll send him to visit."

Vivian Weaver shook her head yes.

Levon and I waved and got into Roger's truck for the drive back to New Orleans. I kept silent on the topic of Levon's mother being long dead.

63

"How'd it go in there?" Roger asked.

"Vivian Weaver doesn't hate you, if that's what you mean. She misses you."

"That's just a ploy on her part to get me back in that house. She doesn't know it yet, but I'm never setting foot in there again. Not ever."

"Then why did you pick us up?"

Roger took his eyes off the road.

"Would you want to get on that woman's bad side? I do whatever she wants and I hope that she doesn't call on me too often for too many favors. And that's the whole truth. How's your arm, anyway?"

"Better."

"How much blood did it cost you?"

"None. Yet."

"That's unusual. Vivian Weaver's a collector of the stuff. Sometimes she says it's for a neighbor's sick child. Other times it's for old Simon Hellion's cancer treatment down the road. It all depends on what she thinks will work on your particular mind."

I looked over at Levon.

"So what does she do with the blood?"

"What do you think she does with it?" Roger asked. "She keeps it for herself that's what. It keeps her young and energetic. That's what she tells me."

"I don't care. I like Vivian Weaver and she can have my blood if she wants it."

"Oh, you better not say that too loud or she'll come calling for you real soon. You owe her now that she fixed your arm. You're in her loop."

Levon grabbed the sleeve of my shirt and pulled me toward him. "We can't leave until you give her a gift," he said. "You'll get sick again. You have to give her something she needs in her life."

"How about money?"

"No. She needs that, but not so bad."

"Just tell me what it is, Levon."

"Give her blood. I can tell you for sure that if you donated, it would make her happy."

"I will, okay? I'll send it to her."

"You better," said Levon. "If you don't your wrist is gonna go right back to the way it was before."

I didn't tell either of them that I was taking Levon back home with me, but I knew it was my freedom card from Vivian Weaver. She would never bother me as long as I was taking care of her grandson. I looked back at him. He was staring out the window, sucking up all the scenery around his old grandma's house.

"You've been awfully quiet, kid," Roger said to Levon. "You're not gonna sleep the whole way back, are you?"

"No. I'm not tired right now. I've been sitting back here thinking that it's time for Evangeline to pick a card."

I rested my chin on the back of my seat and looked at the black deck Levon had spread across the seat cushion.

"Come on. Pick one."

"You know how I feel about that black deck."

"It's nothing to be afraid of. It's just asking you to look at the dark side of things. Like midnight and moonlight and shiny black lake water and all the space between all the stars. You're getting better at it too. In New Orleans I had to be really careful with you."

"You asked me to go to a cemetery for you. What was careful about that?"

I leaned across the seat and chose a card.

"Are you sure you want that one?"

"Obviously you want me to choose another one."

For the first time since I'd begun choosing cards way back with Rosemary in Cyril, I did not stick with my original choice, but picked a different card.

"People don't change their minds often enough," said Levon. "They think it's a weakness, but it's a real lifesaver."

I knew the drill. I handed Levon the new card without looking at it. He studied it without a single change in his expression.

"Ever think about playing poker?" I asked.

"I've played a few hands in my day."

"Your day? You're fourteen years old. You haven't had a day."

Levon stared at my card as if I weren't speaking. As if I weren't even in the same car with him. Vivian Weaver was right. He was gifted. He gave nothing away.

When he finally spoke it was in a monotone, trancelike voice.

"Once you were a fool and now you're still a fool," he said.

"I pulled the Fool?"

"No. Your card is the Lovers."

"You don't sound happy."

"It's your card, why should I be happy?"

"I mean you don't sound like you like the card."

"It's a card about making decisions. Nobody ever likes making decisions."

"In love?"

"Yep. Some people say it's about choosing between two lovers, but I think that's a simple interpretation."

"What do you think?"

"I think it's about choosing to be with someone who's difficult to love. It's about not being scared of another person. Not making the simpler choice. And not choosing the easy road out of fear."

"Are you saying it's a heart-over-mind thing?" said Roger. "That's always a mistake."

"It depends," said Levon. "Some people's instincts got all twisted up when they were kids and they shouldn't trust themselves. But most people's instincts are right on the money."

Roger stared at Levon through the rearview mirror and I stared at him over the backseat.

"Are you saying I should choose Michael over Gabriel because he's more difficult?"

"I'm not saying anything. It's your card, not mine. I doubt I would've picked such a confusing card. And besides, I don't know about your love affairs, I'm just your neighbor. All I know is that you're going to have to make a choice real soon."

"Pick the easier guy," said Roger. "It's all about sex with the difficult ones. When you're older and the heat dies down you might not have anything to talk about. The easier one, the one it wasn't so hot with, he'll always be your friend."

"It was hot with both of them."

"That's a lie you're telling yourself."

I closed my eyes. I was not going to take Roger's advice on love or Levon's either. Instead, I listened to the static on the radio. The music was incredible in Louisiana, but the reception was terrible so the radio was a tease. Road pornography. A beautiful note here and there, just enough to keep you tuned in, static and all.

"See those dark clouds? There's a storm coming up ahead," said Roger.

The waiting was torturous, but when they came the drops fell like a hail of gunfire in large, loud, deadly precision onto the steel roof of the truck. I clenched my fists.

"Are you all right, Evangeline? Afraid of the rain?"

"I don't like the sound of the raindrops."

"Well, just so you know, we're heading into a downpour and I'm not about to stop driving anytime soon. I gotta be in New Orleans in two hours."

I opened the glove compartment, took out a tissue, ripped it in half, rolled the pieces into little balls, and stuck them in my ears. It dulled the sound of the drops and pretty soon it was raining so hard I couldn't hear each one separately anyway. I took the paper out and the rain sounded less like bullets and more like a pulse, like a drumbeat, a heartbeat. As if the truck had a bloodstream all its own.

64

I stood in front of the house on Magazine Street memorizing its soft lilac color, not blue and not purple, its sunken steps, its chipped

porch, and its lace-patterned ironwork balconies. I locked the
details into my mind, knowing that I'd most likely never see them
again in real life.

I walked up to the porch, but I was afraid to go inside. I'd left
Michael without supplies, so to speak, without a way to make all
those paintings he had gotten commissions for at the gallery show.
It must have been humiliating for him to tell his customers that he
would not be able to paint their portraits, or that if he did, they
would not feel the same way about his work as when they first saw
it at the opening.

I knocked softly. And then with more force. He didn't answer
and I took it as a sign that I ought to move away from the instruc-
tions of Vivian Weaver and back into my own life. I started down
the porch steps with the idea that I would stop in at Johnny River's
across the street, say goodbye to the waitress there, and then head
home to the safety of New York and the Stone Crow. But Michael
called to me from the doorway before I reached the sidewalk.

He looked terribly thin and haggard, with dark circles under his
eyes and an unshaven face. I went up to him and touched his beard.

"What happened to you?" I asked.

"You know what happened," he said.

"You can't paint?"

"Not a stroke."

He stepped aside and I walked back into the house I had sworn
I would never go inside of again. There were canvases in the middle of the living room, sitting in the fountain, water dripping over
them. Ruined. Paint had seeped into the antique rugs and the pale
pink loveseats. Also ruined.

"Why?" I asked.

"They are no good without you. I'm a terrible, terrible painter.
Much worse than I thought. When you left I came to that realization and I destroyed them all."

I took his hand and walked through the trashed living room to
the back of the house and the painting studio. As we passed his

bedroom I saw metal pipes lying on the floor underneath the carved pastel Madonna, who looked down on them with great pity.

"I removed them from under the sink in the bathroom," he said. "I scraped them for your hairs. Any last ones I could find."

"How did you do it?"

"With a flashlight and long tweezers."

He was past embarrassment, desperation, irony. He was deadened, honest, and serious.

We continued on to his studio. It had been turned upside down. Paint on the floors and the church pews, shredded canvas, splintered wooden frames, and a broken mirror so broken it had no glass left inside of it at all.

"I was angry," he said.

"At me?"

"At both of us. At myself, mostly, for believing that I could become famous without any actual talent."

"It was a brilliant idea in its own way. And it did work, at least for a while. I'm sure you can live forever on the sale of those thirty paintings."

"The scent will fade from them in time. Even with the addition of the blue lotus. Their owners will come to hate them. To view them as a waste of money. I'll be found out and subject to humiliation beyond my imagining."

"You could take the money and leave New Orleans," I said. "It would be okay to do that."

"You can't possibly understand, Evangeline. I wanted to be a great painter. More than anything else, more than love or money, I wanted greatness. I wanted a place in history. I could never understand why God gave you such a gift while he gave me nothing. I thought you were wasting God's work. I thought I was doing the right thing by taking it from you and that God would reward me for my ingenuity and resourcefulness."

"No you didn't. You never thought any of those things."

Michael looked around his studio.

"No, I didn't."

"I'm going to give you what you want, Michael. I'm going to give you everything."

He looked stunned.

"We did this together. I paid with my relationship with Gabriel and you paid with your pride and your realization about who you really are and what your true place is in the world of artists. We are going to finish what we started and then I'm going to walk away. And I never want to see you again. And you will not ask and I will not owe you anything."

"Why would you do this for me?"

"Because I want freedom. I want a clean slate. I don't want you to come after me for what I have. And don't tell me you won't because I know that you will. And you know it too."

"It's true. I won't lie to you," he said. "I was already planning it."

"I'm going to make you famous, endlessly and ultimately famous, and I know how to do that now, but then you need to walk away and you need to let me do the same. Can you do that?"

"I can."

"You don't love me, Michael."

"No. I don't love anyone."

"That's right. And you have to remember that every time you think of me. Every time your greed surfaces and you want more of me, you have to remember that you have no love and that it would be unfair of you to take mine."

He put his arms around me and looked into my eyes.

"I will remember. I don't love you. I know that."

I slipped out of his arms but not before moving more deeply into them first.

"Wait for me in the bathroom," I said.

I went back into the great room in the front of the house and searched through the rubble of his work for a glass. On the fireplace mantel I saw a crystal goblet. A ray of afternoon sunlight coming in through the drapes hit the cut glass and threw multi-colored beams of light onto the sofa and the floor. I looked sadly at the rainbow patterns floating across the room. It was God's work, and the colors in Michael's paintings would never come close. His own mind could never dream up such beauty.

I brought the goblet back to the bathroom and placed it on the sink.

"Do you want me to run the bath one last time?" he asked.

He sounded childlike and so hopeful.

"No," I said. "I want you to be silent, and thankful, and try not to draw me any further into your world."

I opened the medicine cabinet and took the silver razor from the kit.

"Don't be scared. I'm going to give you a parting gift."

"I am scared. I'm scared of the word 'parting.' Please don't use it when you talk about us."

"Parting. Say the word," I said. "Say it over and over again. Say it until you're used to it, because there is no us. There never was. It was always only Gabriel and me."

I sounded convincing but I knew that I was speaking as much to myself as I was to Michael.

"Are you ready for fame and fortune?" I asked.

"I am," he said.

I did not give myself time to think. As he nodded his head I sliced the razor over my arm, connecting the two puncture wounds with a line so straight it looked like a surgical cut. Gabriel would have been proud.

My skin opened up with the single slash and I took the ruby vial from my pocket and filled it with a special gift for Vivian Weaver. Blood poured out into the tiny vial and then the shallow crystal goblet.

The scent of my blood was mesmerizing in its intensity, a luscious, potent, ethereal haze that clung to the walls of the bathroom. It was far more intense than the opening of the vial itself. It was like a thousand ruby red vials. A million. It filled the room like an actual presence, and it dawned on us both at the same time that my blood not only contained the scent, but was the scent itself.

Leather, like warm Egyptian incense, like a dark library in an old city.

Jasmine, like the sweet, sweet scent of decay.

Fire, like hot darkness.

And red velvet rose, like a sheath of light and lilting femininity.

I exuded. There was no other verb for what was happening in Michael Bon Chance's bathroom. And the scent was pure. Not created inside a laboratory for use on the body, but made by the body for the body. The body itself was the laboratory, the blood the perfume.

"It was God's work after all," said Michael, awe seeping into his voice. "You were simply born this way."

꒕

I put my arm to my face, not caring if the blood spread onto my cheeks. My birthright was so beautiful I would have bathed in it if I felt I could sustain the loss.

"Use it sparingly," I whispered.

"Evangeline, please."

"It's more powerful than my nails, or skin, or hair, or even my tears. I'm giving it to you because I love you, even though you could never love me back. I don't blame you for that. And I don't feel sorry for you either. It's what you are. It's how you're made. Just as this scent is how I'm made."

The drops from my wrist slowed down and the sound of them hitting the bottom of the glass, one by one, was hard to take. I pressed on my forearm to hasten the process, but the blood would not come down fast enough. All of a sudden I realized that every drop I'd ever heard, from the sweat of Gabriel's forehead in the white room to the endless rain in New Orleans, all of it had been imitating the drops of blood falling into the crystal goblet, hinting at the origin and truth of my scent.

꒱

"Michael, you're going to have to do something for me."

"Anything."

And of course I knew that he would do anything for me now.

"We are going into the bedroom. You are going to lie on the bed and I'm going to put my head over your lap. I'll need you to hold it steady."

"Okay."

"You're going to take the razor and slice the part of my neck over the mark from the ruby vial. Don't think about it too hard, or too long, just pass the blade gently over the skin to open it. When the blood begins to flow, hold the goblet under the wound and collect as much of it as you can."

65

Michael sat on the bed with his neck against the headboard of the carved pastel Madonna and I lay horizontally across his body. To the winged angels painted on the baby blue ceiling we must have looked like a human crucifix.

He moved my hair behind my ears in just the same way that Gabriel had and then he lifted my head and held the razor over my neck.

"I don't know if I can," he said.

"You have to. Think of yourself. Do it for yourself."

I knew that would get to him—he was good at putting his own

needs first—and I was right. He placed the blade against my neck and made the cut directly over the mark of the red vial.

The scent was strong once again and this time I tried to bathe my senses in it, as I doubted that I would ever again have the experience of being enveloped in the perfume of my own existence.

I looked up and from my vantage point Michael seemed to be dreaming. I feared that my blood would go to waste.

"Wake up, Michael. Stop staring and place the goblet under the wound."

"My God, Evangeline, the beauty of your blood is staggering. You have to leave as soon as we're done," he said. "If you stay I won't be able to resist you. I'll kill you for what's inside of you. I'm sure that I will."

I felt drowsy as the blood flowed out.

"I have to, Evangeline," he said, and then he leaned over and put his mouth on my neck and I felt the sucking pull of his lips and tongue, as if he were trying to drag my heart out of my chest with his mouth.

With all the strength I had I pulled his face toward mine and put my mouth on his. He would have taken every last drop of blood that he could get from my veins if I hadn't. He would have done it for the intimacy, the only form of it that he could understand. He was greedy and he would never have been able to stop himself. I kissed him for the second time since I'd known him, but this time I did it for the right reason. I did it to save my own life.

The soft girlish quality of the red velvet rose and the masculinity of the leather were incredibly arousing, and once we started there was no pulling us apart. He was on top of me and then inside of me. The sheets were soaked with blood. The mattress stained beyond repair. The scent incredible. Jasmine and rose. Fire and leather and the bitter brine of tears. The room would never be rid of it. It would have to be burned down to be free of us.

When we were done I noticed that the glass goblet had been carefully placed back on the nightstand to avoid a loss. Ah, Michael, still thinking of himself even during the highest moments of his passion. True to himself to the very end.

We lay like that for hours. This time it was Michael who refused to get up and shower, exactly the way I had been with Gabriel way back in another lifetime.

I knew that when I left he was going to paint covered in my blood. I knew that he would wet his body and run a brush across it and use my very insides on his canvas. Every drop he could get. I also knew that I had to wake myself up and get out of the house. I was in danger. He would try to persuade me to give him more until little by little I would become too weak to move. So weak that he could keep me next to him for the rest of what would be a very short life.

66

I stayed in Michael's bed until it was nighttime. When I had regained some strength I went into the bathroom to wash. I ran a bath, dried myself off, and got dressed. My clothes were on the floor, making a trail from the bathroom to the bedroom, but at least they were clean and untouched.

I knew that Michael was in his studio painting, mixing the contents of the crystal goblet into his colors. Starting on the new works he had been paid for. He hadn't even bothered to ask if I wanted anything, not a glass of water or a cup of coffee. He had already gone back to his one true love.

Saying goodbye to him was not painful. We were part of each other now. My blood was in his body, part of his stream, part of him. I had given him what he wanted most and I felt satisfied with that. I had completed the circle with him and I was finished. I knew he would eventually want me again, but I had his promise to leave me alone, and the layer of protection from Vivian Weaver.

Standing in the studio watching him paint, I tried to understand the love and affection he had for the canvas, so much more powerful than for any human being. I tried not to judge him for loving an inanimate object so deeply. I was not a painter. I didn't pretend to know what he was feeling.

He could not pull his eyes off his work. Although I'm sure he knew I was standing there, he had a stronger drive to finish a particular stroke, or to let a drop of paint fall just so, than to speak to me.

"I'm leaving," I said.

"I'll never see you again, will I?" he said, without looking up from his easel.

"You won't."

"You've chosen Gabriel. He's the more prosaic choice, but I don't hold it against you."

I did not want to argue, or even speak about Gabriel. I did not want to betray him any more than I already had. I said nothing but he continued on.

"Well, the choice is yours, of course," he said, "but I think you're making the wrong one. You can have an interesting life with an artist, or a boring one with a doctor who you will never see because he'll be at the hospital at all hours, just like he is already. That's the reason you were with me, you know. Loneliness. He was never there for you in the first place."

"The interest level of my life doesn't depend on the job of the man I'm with."

"Really? I don't see you doing anything special with your own life."

"That's because you don't notice anything except yourself."

"If you say so."

"You want me here for yourself only, Michael, for your paintings and the success of your career, and you know that. True, it was my loneliness that brought us together, but it was also your selfishness.

It was the combination. You are never going to see me again. Do you understand that?"

He finally put his brush down. He stepped away from his easel and put his arms around me. He held me tight and kissed the mark on my neck.

"You'll come back to me," he whispered.

I stood frozen in his arms. I felt immobilized, terrified of the passion I felt for him that was never, ever going to go away. I had to get out right then, at that moment, and never turn around.

He took his arms from my body and stood with them at his sides, staring at me. He walked backward, slowly, stretching time, keeping his eyes on mine, until he was in front of his easel once more. He picked up his brush and looked away.

I walked out of the room. He did not watch me go because somewhere in his mind he still thought I was coming back.

And maybe he was right.

&

I stopped at Johnny River's on the way home for a last look at the lilac Victorian across the street. I took a seat at the counter and waited to see if Michael would come outside and try to find me. Of course he didn't, and I should not have expected him to.

I admitted to myself from the safety of the diner that what we had done together was the most intimate act I had shared with anyone in my life. If I ever saw Gabriel again, I would make him taste my blood, and I his. Tasting the inside of someone else's body brought more closeness than kissing or even lovemaking.

"You look far away, Eggs, like you've been on vacation or something."

"I wish I were, but I'm right here on Magazine Street."

"What happened to your neck? It looks pretty bad, like an animal got to you."

I'd forgotten about my neck. It had looked okay to me in Michael's bathroom mirror but it probably wasn't ready to be seen by anyone else.

"I can handle the gore, but I'm not sure they can," she said, looking out over the customers.

I covered the side of my neck with my hair while she placed coffee and eggs in front of me.

"Was it the Magician that did it?"

"It was the Lovers."

"Be careful. You don't want to end up in a mental institution like the last woman who got involved with him. You know the story. That couple told it to you last time you were here. Someday some couple is going to be in here talking about you and how you thought you were going to be special to that painter from across the street and how you ended up just like the rest of the women who got involved with him."

I went to pay, but the waitress put her hand on my forearm.

"Consider yourself warned. And the eggs are on me."

67

The apartment on St. Louis was blessedly quiet. I went into the bathroom and studied my neck in the mirror. It was hard to calculate how much had happened since the day the vial touched my skin, but it was true that every single thing in my life had changed, just as Louise had said it would.

I washed my face and lay down in the living room to rest. Michael had not drained me, at least not physically, as Vivian Weaver was afraid he might, but he had weakened me more than a little.

I thought of Gabriel, my doctor of the dead. Two days had already passed since I'd been back from the Bayou Jolie and still no sign of him. I was resigned to it. If I was ever with him again I would be less careless. I doubted that I would get the chance, but if I did I would treat him like a necklace of sapphires.

I found the strength to go upstairs. I stripped the linens off the bed, took my clothes off, pulled all of Gabriel's things out of the closet, and threw everything into the wash. While the laundry was going, I packed the rest of my things for the trip to Cyril. Organizing gave me a feeling of setting things straight. Of making things normal once again, like righting the upside-down Magician.

The washing and cleaning made me think of my mother. She loved doing those things. She said it took her mind off her worries. In truth she wasn't very good at it. Everything she touched ended up smelling like cigarette smoke, and all of my clothes had smudge marks from where she dropped her ash during the folding or the ironing.

But ever since I discovered the origins of my scent I could not help but think of her in a different way. After all, it had come from her blood and her body and had been passed on to me by her. If our bloodline was all we had in common, as she had so often told me, then it was enough for me. I didn't exactly miss her, but I loved her. How could I not? After all, she had given me the fire and the leather, the jasmine and the red velvet rose. In a sense she had given me Gabriel, Michael, Levon, and Vivian Weaver. With all she had given to me so long ago when she made me, it was easy to pick up the phone and call.

ぷ

"Mom."

"Evangeline! Is that you?"

"You know it is."

"How are you doing, sweetheart?"

I tensed. She had never called me that before.

"I'm good."

"How's college?"

"College?"

"You told me you were going down south to look at colleges, remember? Do you like LSU?"

I loved my mother even more just then as I realized that she actually believed the things I'd told her.

"Mom, you don't even know what LSU is."

"So you're not going?"

"I'm coming home tomorrow. Well, not home, but I'll be back in Cyril."

"I'll come up to visit."

"I've got a friend with me. A kid. He's fourteen."

"Evangeline!"

I rolled my eyes. Only my mother could think something like that.

"I'm taking care of him, Mom. He's my neighbor and he has no mother."

"Yes I do," said Levon. I turned around and he was standing right behind me.

"Shush," I said to him. "I'm on the phone."

"I don't care. I have a mother."

"Hold on a second, Mom.

"Vivian Weaver told me. It's okay, Levon."

"I have a mother. She's dead, but she's still my mother."

He had a point.

"I'm sorry. You do have a mother. Everyone does."

I said goodbye to my own mother and looked at Levon, all blond hair down to his waist, intense black eyes, and jeans low on his hips. He was leaning against the bedroom door frame and I could picture him years from now, at twenty-four or -five, saying goodbye to some poor, unfortunate, weeping girl, in the same exact stance.

I went over to him, not sure how to act in front of all that sudden sultry teenaged distance and slight disdain.

I touched his shoulder and he stepped back.

"Why didn't you tell me you lived alone?"

"I'm fine by myself."

"What about the finger? You made me take it to the cemetery for your mother's arthritis."

"I was paying my respects. She loved to paint her nails red. It's really all I can remember about her anymore. I would have done it myself, but it makes me sad sometimes when I go there. I figured you were a good stand-in."

"I know you can take care of yourself, Levon, but you must get lonely sometimes?"

"I took care of you too, not just myself."

"Yes, you did. And I'd like to repay the favor by asking you to come stay with me in New York."

"I've never been to New York. I don't know if they would like my type up there."

"Oh, I think they would like your type pretty much anywhere."

"Would I have to go to school?"

"Probably."

"I'd have to bring all my stuff."

"You don't have that much stuff. Vivian Weaver said she would take the cabinet of curiosities. She can use some of the items to help heal her clients."

That was a lie, but there was no way that cabinet from hell was coming back to Cyril.

"I'll miss the ceramic fingers and locks of hair," he said. "I took care of them for a long time."

"I have other things you can take care of in New York."

"I doubt it. You're not the kind who would put too much time into those types of things. You would look after them when you wanted to and then stop when you didn't feel like it anymore."

"I'm not going to stop caring for you, Levon. You're my family now. I got cured by your old grandma."

"You're not there yet. Not until you send her some of your blood."

I shook my head. I had the ruby glass vial all ready to send to Vivian Weaver.

"Pack your stuff," I said. "I rented a car and we're leaving early. Do you need me to wake you up?"

"No, I'm a morning person by nature."

A morning person living around all that darkness made me think that Levon would be very happy in Cyril and away from the darkness of the Quarter.

"Evangeline, am I moving, or just visiting?"

"I hope you'll stay forever, Levon. But you can stay as long as you like."

68

Levon kept his head out the window on the mountain road up to Cyril.

"It smells good out here, Evangeline," he yelled, "even better than you."

"Pine needles," I yelled back, "from the evergreen trees."

"There must be a lot of animals out here?"

"Some."

"Wolves?"

"There are wolves, yes, but they don't come into the town very often."

"Does your friend Michael?"

"No."

Levon sat back in his seat.

"I could read the cards and tell you whether or not he's gonna come for you."

"No. That's fine. I'll deal with it if it happens."

"When it happens," he said, "and it will. These things always do."

"They do in New Orleans," I said. "It's different here."

Levon sighed as if he were an old man and I were a young child.

We drove in silence. Levon took in the sight of the forest and I thought about how I was never going to get away from New Orleans. How I could already feel it creeping up behind me. And how I knew it was forever going to reach its weird, bony hand into my life from across all the states in between us. I switched on the radio. The sad, haunting sound of the oboe floated into the car.

"It's the nature of life for things to sound that way," said Levon.

We drove down the main street of Cyril, turned right, and pulled up in front of the Stone Crow. I sat in the car with my seat belt on. I had the feeling that it was holding my life together. That if I took it off everything would fall down around me.

Levon was already out of the car. He came around to my side and stuck his head in the window.

"Is this where you grew up?"

"Part of the time."

"It looks cold."

"It's the kind of place that needs people to warm it up."

"Maybe we should turn around and go back to New Orleans. It's warm there all the time."

I thought about the cold, cold hands of Michael Bon Chance.

69

Between Levon and me we had two bags and a deck of black-backed tarot cards. We were traveling light except for an overload of the psyche, which we were both familiar with but for different reasons. I knew what my own baggage was, but I was sure I did not even know the half of Levon's.

I pushed the heavy front door hard, with my shoulder, until it opened.

"You should fix that," said Levon, standing behind me. "I don't see myself living in a place that's hard to get into."

"Maybe you can fix it. It'll be your fall project."

"My project is making sure you don't fall apart."

The house felt warmer inside than it looked on the outside. The same as always, the Stone Crow was like a stern person with a kind heart.

As I walked down the front hallway I ran my fingertips along the wall, feeling for memories of Louise in the stone. A light was on in the kitchen and I could smell burning wood from the fireplace in the great room. I left my suitcase where I stood and walked toward the light.

Once again, just as it had been so long ago, it was a shock to see the boy from the coffee shop. The one with the tight, pale skin, and the long dark hair. He was sitting at the table surrounded by books and papers spread out all around him, as though he'd been there for a long, long time.

"You're here," I said.

"For a while now," said Gabriel. "I couldn't work in New Orleans and it was just so quiet here."

"I remember you," said Levon. "You're the boyfriend. You passed by me on the stairway and never said a word."

"Sorry," said Gabriel. "I was in too much of a rush to notice anybody but myself."

I looked at his black hair, longer now, with waves that broke the line of its previously straight simplicity.

"Levon." I pointed at the door.

"I know," he said. "I'm gone."

I wished he hadn't phrased it that way.

I turned to Gabriel.

"Are you back, or just here for right now?"

"Just here," he said. "There's no going back."

"I understand."

"I'm not so sure you do."

Gabriel had a cynical, amused look that I had never seen on his face. And in that one second of his new, hostile smile I saw that I had aged him. Loving me had jaded him and taken something away, some quality he had had since he was a child.

"Do you know what it's like to love someone like you?" he said.

"I don't."

"You look right past the men who love you in search of the ones who don't. It was as if you could only see me when I was with Rayanne, before I fell in love with you. The minute I loved you, you were done with me. Finished."

"It wasn't like that."

"You slipped away from me whenever you felt like it and came back whenever you wanted. At first I liked that about you, the slipperiness, the scent, the strangeness of it, the white room, the dreams of Louise, everything. Every single day with you was like an amusement park ride. And that scent. Oh my God. Even though I'm a doctor I could never take it apart and put it back together again. I couldn't decipher it or figure out where it came from and I liked that. But I always thought that things would become normal someday. Like this was the beginning part, but the middle and the end would be more solid. But the thing is, you don't ever get more solid."

"I made mistakes, Gabriel. I got pulled into places I didn't understand. It's a long story, what happened between Michael and me, and it isn't as simple as you're trying to make it. Don't you want the truth?"

"I know the truth," he said. "It was laid out in every single painting in every single room in that gallery on Royal Street. The truth wasn't hard to figure out, Evangeline. Only the reasons for it."

"I didn't love him. I desired him, I did, I won't lie, but I never,

ever loved him. And he didn't love me either. And that's as true as the paintings on the wall."

"I know it is," he said in a change of tone. "I know."

He stood up and went to the refrigerator.

"When I came back to the Stone Crow the scent of you was everywhere. The house was so filled with you that I went from room to room, sure you were in here somewhere."

Gabriel put his hair behind his ears the way he used to do with mine.

"Then I found this," he said. He opened the door to the freezer and picked up the ice-cube tray that Louise had used to make the bloodsicles so many years ago, now melted red and watery. He held up the bloody washcloth that she had saved and put next to the ice tray when I was ten years old and I immediately touched the scar on my forehead where I had cut it open sleepwalking.

"When we left for New Orleans they turned off the electricity in the house. The ice cubes thawed out in the freezer and that's what I smelled when I came into the house. I knew the truth about you then. The truth was in your plasma and your cells, your escino-phils, neutrophils, and platelets. It was in your blood. Louise didn't make the scent, she only collected it and then gave it back to you inside of the ruby vial."

"She took it from me when I was just a little girl," I said. "A healer on the bayou told me, in her own way." I looked toward the beautiful blond boy in the living room, amazed that I had ever met him at all. "It was Levon's grandmother, Vivian Weaver."

"I can understand what Michael wanted," said Gabriel. "And I know I brought you to New Orleans and left you alone every day. And I know you were lonely."

As the hours went by Gabriel swung between anger and forgive-ness so many times it was exhausting. He blamed me, he blamed Michael, he blamed himself. I let him believe whatever it was that he needed to believe in any given moment, but the longer I listened to his many tortured versions of our story, the more I knew that there was really only one.

I had been in love with two men at the same time, and one was evil and one was good.

70

"All your faults are visible to me, Evangeline," Gabriel whispered in bed.

"I can smell the jasmine and the rose, the fire and the leather, but now the slight tinge of your blood and the brine of your tears, all the things that make you simply human, are just as clear."

I let him love me. I took his body into mine. I let his dark hair drape over my face like a shiny black tent under which we could look into each other's eyes in privacy.

I looked at the perfect blue star birthmark on his arm, in almost the same place as the puncture wound on my own and I brought it up to my lips. I traced the points with my index finger.

We are the same, I thought. His star and my scent. Both of us in possession of something so perfect and so unique that it did not seem possible that we were born with it, and yet we were.

"Close your eyes, my beautiful angel Gabriel," I said, and then I sang the poem for him, the one that Vivian Weaver had given to me out on the Bayou Jolie.

> *I am your mother,*
> *I can make you a brother.*
> *I'm not in your mind,*
> *I don't exist in your soul,*
> *But you will come to know me,*
> *You will feel it in your bones.*

I sang the song of my blood. It came from my mother, it could make a blood brother, it was not in my mind, and it was not in my soul, but it was made from the very marrow inside of my bones.

So, my name is Eva from the longer and more beautiful Evange-line. I had something very special once, something that I took for granted and lost. I set out to find it again, and as so often happens, it was right there in front of me. Or should I say it was right there inside of me, running through my veins like a blessing, or a plague.

I closed my eyes and dreamed of Louise, an aromata from New Orleans who gave me nothing I did not already have.

ACKNOWLEDGMENTS

Thanks to my friends: Marylu Lambert, Sam Feldman, Grant Collier, Oliver Jolliffe, and Irene Alysandratos.

To my family: Claudia, Anna, Marianne, Al, and especially my mom, Evelyn Berwin, for her love and friendship.

To Armand Dimele, always. To Mark Millar for renting me his apartment in the French Quarter on the cheap. To Stephen Josephson for getting me in the writing mood. And to my father, Milton Berwin, aka Jake, for living his life as an artist and showing me how it's done.

A NOTE ABOUT THE AUTHOR

Margot Berwin is the author of the best-selling novel *Hot-house Flower and the Nine Plants of Desire*. Her work has been translated into nineteen languages. She earned her MFA from the New School in 2005 and lives in New York City.

A NOTE ON THE TYPE

The text of this book was set in Sabon, a typeface designed
by Jan Tschichold (1902–1974). Based on the original designs
by Claude Garamond (ca. 1480–1561), Sabon was named for
the Lyons punch cutter Jacques Sabon, who brought some of
Garamond's matrices to Frankfurt.

Typeset by Scribe, Philadelphia, Pennsylvania

Printed and bound by Berryville Graphics, Berryville, Virginia

Designed by Maggie Hinders